Winston

Peter Tinniswood

ARROW BOOKS

Arrow Books Limited
20 Vauxhall Bridge Road, London SW1V 2SA

An imprint of the Random Century Group

London Melbourne Sydney Auckland
Johannesburg and agencies throughout
the world

First published in Great Britain in 1991 by Hutchinson

This edition published in 1992 by Arrow Books

1 3 5 7 9 10 8 6 4 2

© 1991 by Peter Tinniswood

Printed and bound in Great Britain by
Cox & Wyman Ltd., Reading, Berkshire

ISBN 0 09 915491 9

For my good friend, Maurice Denham

1

Nancy Empson is unmarried.

She is a tall, handsome woman in her mid-forties. She has bold eyes, springy navy-blue hair and her legs are long.

She has a father, a brother called William and a sister called Rosie. When she was a little girl she had a Shetland sheepdog called Wynford.

She lives in the old Dower House in the village of Winterleaf Gunner, which lies deep in a snuck and a snuggle of the smooth-cropped downlands of the West of England.

When she was a little girl she once lived in a thin house with a mournful roof in the east of Scotland.

From her bedroom window she could see the spars of fishing smacks and black guillemots in the winter harbour.

This is the story of her concurrence with Winston, the village poacher.

It started in autumn.

Fieldfare and redwing fluttered clumsily in the gorging hedgerows. The River Florey was fat and flustered. Wrens sang in dense thickets of damp bramble and lead shot barked into the guts of plump and silly pheasants.

2

I adore the autumn.

It's not cocky. It knows its place in the order of things. It doesn't rush you. It isn't pushy.

All the members of my family adore autumn. It makes tiny sobbing noises in our bones. It whispers in our scalps. It lies across our feet in the evenings like a tired and contented spaniel.

William used to collect conkers. Hundreds of them. Thousands. Then he turned his attention to train-spotting. It was the autumn of the age of steam, and I don't think he's ever recovered from it. He writes these silly little books about railways now. That's his profession. Imagine a grown man devoting his whole life to bemoaning the passing of the shunter's pole and the heavy mineral tank locomotive. I think it speaks volumes for the parlous state of public transport in this country, don't you?

Rosie always looks at her best in autumn. I think it suits her colouring. I think it mellows her bad temper. And that, I may say, is no bad thing. Those tantrums! The ranting and the raving and the gnashing of teeth! Quite ghastly.

In the autumn she's much calmer. She smiles softly to herself and she takes fresh-baked teacakes to the ducks on the village pond.

I wonder why? Maybe autumn makes her realize that one day her skin will wrinkle and brown blotches will cluster the backs of her hands and she'll need a pink, dimpled rubber mat in the bottom of her bath.

Maybe the prospect appeals to her. Who knows? Only the great icy void beyond the planets, I suppose.

And as for Father.

Oh, my God, I feel so guilty about him.

Last autumn I killed him off, you see. Stone dead.

I drowned him in the River Florey.

Not in one fell swoop, you understand. He lingered on for a few weeks and then with a weary sigh he gave up the struggle in his best pyjamas.

We had his funeral with the vicar and hymns sung in tune.

I wept among the cypress trees in the graveyard and Winston comforted me.

He put his arm gently round my waist. Gently he drew me into him. Softly he placed his lips close to the smooth, tingly skin at the back of my ears and he whispered:

'There, there, missus, don't you bother your arse over him. The old bugger's best out of it, ain't he? They always is at their age, my old wingsy bash.'

Dear Lord, I killed my father!

Well, not literally.

It was in my imagination.

Well, come on, own up. How many of you have done the same with an elderly parent who's driving you insane, burning holes in your Chinese rug, putting forks the wrong way up in the dishwasher, getting stuck in the wardrobe, smelling of prunes, grumbling incessantly about the new decimal coinage, frightening the bullfinches on the bird table, dropping fragments of All Bran on to your roll of Sellotape, just being indescribably, shamelessly, relentlessly old?

How many of you have lain awake at nights plotting the death of your mother or your father?

A swift and painless garrotting on the grille at the old-age pension counter at the local sub-post office. A coach with a bald off-side front tyre crashing on the motorway on an Old Folks' outing to Hastings. An untimely tumble over a discarded spectacle case in the optician's waiting room. A frenzied, unprovoked attack by a drug-crazed trainee chiropodist. The bullet of a hired assassin with a silencer on his Mauser, and a toothbrush moustache and gold front teeth and strands of greasy black hair stretched tautly across a bald, olive-skinned pate and wide lapels on a tight-waisted black and white striped suit.

Nothing happens.

They live on.

Tirelessly, tenaciously, ruthlessly they live on.

And so does Father.

Oh my crikey, oh my golly, how he lives on.

Father who has dedicated his whole life to making our existence utterly miserable, totally wretched.

Father moving us from pillar to post the length and breadth of the country at the merest whiff of his whims and fancies.

Father boring us to distraction with his interminable stories about his days in the army and his adventures in India.

Father guzzling up our youth and our happiness and our freedom like a blind and bloated lamprey.

Father demanding our love and our grief and our despair and our frustration.

Father, above all, demanding our time which is slipping through our fumbling fingers as our spring withers, our summer shrivels and our autumn stutters into our long, slow winter.

Winter, please don't come.

Let it always be autumn.

Please, please, please.

I adore the autumn.

3

We were sitting in the drawing room of the old Dower House at Winterleaf Gunner.

We had just finished an early dinner out of the freezer.

When you live in the country you always seem to be eating meals out of the freezer.

I swear I shall scream if I see another fish finger. I shall throw myself naked on to the Chinese rug, and tar and feather myself on the spot if ever again I come face to face with a packet of frozen leaf spinach or a special offer of pre-packed lamb cutlets.

You always seem to be stocking up when you live in the country.

You never buy one box of matches. You buy a whole carton.

You never buy a single bottle of inexpensive wine. You buy a case.

The drawers in your kitchen are always bursting with night lights and balls of garden twine and packets of doilies and Bacofoil and rolls of bin liners and waterproof Elastoplast.

You're terrified of running out.

Sometimes at night when I'm reading my latest well-written book from the library I get petrified that my reading glasses are going to run out of vision.

It was early evening.

They were still preparing the weather forecast for the wireless.

The french doors were wide open and the sun was beating down on the garden, pestering the reluctant roses, snarling at the lawn and scouring the tongues of the dear, uncomplaining French marigolds.

Swallows were swooping at the gables of the old stable, reluctant to set forth on their long salt-spit voyage across the oceans and the dry-mouthed deserts.

Who'd be a swallow?

I would – especially when we run out of ginger nut biscuits for Father's supper.

Midges spiralled above the parch-fingered bower of clematis, coal tits chivied the conifers and the garden robin was singing its head off, bloodthirsty little swine.

What an autumn.

It just would not give in.

If it were a cocker spaniel, and you threw sticks for it, it would have gone on all night long till it dropped dead from exhaustion.

I adore dogs. They've no idea of the future, have they?

We were silent, content, self-contained, each of us immersed in our own singularity.

Rosie was putting the finishing touches to her latest fabric design. That's what she does for a living. She designs fabrics. I think they're very nice, if you like that sort of thing.

Her blonde hair, set free to her shoulders, glowed and the tip of her tongue peeked between her lips as she concentrated on her work.

I could just imagine her rampant in the bed of an unfaithful chartered surveyor from Surrey with a dowdy wife and two adopted dyslexic children from Vietnam.

William sat quietly in a corner next to the drinks tray and the walnut veneer display cabinet listening to train noises on his Walkman and playing with his executive mail-order ball bearings.

Father dozed into his pipe, idly picking at the rim of an empty carton of gentleman's relish resting smugly on the lap of his plus fours.

And I, *moi*, good old Nancy?

Well, I sat in the rocker Mother had won in the golf tournament at Hoylake on the Wirral all those years ago, crocheting a new top for my old tennis dress and making up shopping lists in my mind.

What did I need? What were the essentials for a happy, contented life?

An airship to whisk me away silently to the soaring, snow-sodden peaks of the Andes? A galleon, timbers creaking, spars groaning, sails thrashing, laden to the gunwales with sensuous spices from the Orient and unguents from the swaying tropics to glisten your thighs and tauten your nipples and slither your heaving buttocks? A case of pine-fresh lavatory cleanser?

Suddenly an army helicopter roared and clattered low overhead.

The noise of its rotors hammered into every nook and cranny. It tore at our eardrums and pounded at our breastbones and clutched at our throats.

Father looked up placidly from his carton of gentleman's relish and said with a benign smile:

'I say, helicopters again. Whacko. Jolly Dee. I do love helicopters.

'And look, chaps, you can see the soldiers leaning out and peering through their binoculars.

'Fearfully stirring sight, eh, Rosie?'

Rosie did not look up from her work.

She said very softly:

'My word, yes, Father. Sends the pulses throbbing. Patriotism runs riot, doesn't it?'

Father nodded happily.

And then Rosie looked up and said:

'Listen to me, sunshine, do you know what our brave boys are looking for through their binoculars?'

'No, old boy,' said Father. 'What?'

'Women sunbathing topless in their back gardens.'

William sighed deeply through his sinuses and said:

'I wish you wouldn't be so cynical about everything, Rosie.'

'I'm not being cynical, William. It's true. And it's a bloody disgrace. If you'd got any spunk about you, you'd write to their commanding officer and complain.'

William flushed. He rattled his ball bearings, tugged at the hem of his oatmeal cardigan and said:

'I've got far more important things to do with my life than write letters to gin-sodden, damp-toothed, hen-pecked army officers.'

Rosie rustled her drawing paper angrily and snapped:

'You make me sick.'

'Oh, shut up,' said William.

Little nerves in his neck started to twitch. His lips began to quiver.

13

He opened his mouth, but before he could speak the helicopter zoomed and zackered over the house again, rattling the ivory elephants on the mantelpiece, clinking the ice cubes in the pitcher on the drinks tray and sending the house spider scuttling back to its hole in the skirting board.

Father smiled again and said:

'Fearfully interesting brutes, helicopters. Did I ever tell you about the auto gyro pilot your mother and I met when she was alive and we were living in Pondicherry?

'He told us he hailed from Perpignan, but I doubt it very much. I can't imagine anyone in his right mind wanting to hail from Perpignan. Frightful place. Full of lizards and women with fat bottoms.

'Did I ever tell you about the time your mother and I . . .'

I could sense the screams half-strangled deep in the throats of William and Rosie. I could feel the hatred oozing between their toes and congealing in their armpits.

I switched off. Completely.

I had seen it all before.

Many, many times.

We are what is called a happy family. Contented. Calm. Self-centred. Secure.

Some bloody hopes – and that's using bad language.

How I'd love to live by the side of a frozen lough and feed the wild geese with suet.

How I'd love to live in a back-to-back terraced house in the North of England with a black-lead range and a man sitting by the hearth in industrial boots and sullen braces and the firelight flickering on his naked chest.

Some bloody hopes – and that's still using bad language.

We moved into Winterleaf Gunner from London a year ago; Father, William, Rosie and, of course, myself, Nancy.

Good old Nancy.

Nancy, the arch wiper-up of pee stains. Nancy, the scourge of tide marks round the bath. Nancy, the Genghis Khan of the toilet roll dispenser.

On our first day in the old Dower House we had a major gas leak

14

– twenty-two per cent and rising. And the central heating boiler was condemned, too. Poor little thing. I felt so sorry for it.

On the second day the ceiling in William's study fell in. Then all the pipes burst and we discovered we had to have the whole house rewired. Immediately. At once, if we didn't want to be electrocuted, which thankfully no one did.

We could not have managed without Winston.

Without Winston we would have been completely and utterly defeated.

'Nancy! Nancy!'

I awoke from my reveries with a start.

Isn't reveries a lovely word? You'd like to parcel it up in Christmas paper and send it to a refugee from the Sudan.

I looked up from my crocheting. Rosie was staring at me. There was a sharp glint in her eyes. Her lips were drawn back tightly over her teeth.

Oh crumbs, I thought, another tantrum. What's in store for me now?

I smiled sweetly and I said:

'Yes, Rosie? Anything the matter?'

'Yes,' said Rosie. 'You've got that bloody awful saintly smile on your face again. I can't stand it when you look saintly.'

I smiled again and said quietly:

'I've been thinking about Winston.'

Immediately Rosie's face softened. Her eyes glowed warmly. The moisture returned to her lips. 'Winston,' she said. 'Lovely, lovely man with his fat brown belly and his droopy Zapata moustache and the blue-chipped vein between his two front teeth.'

'Hear, hear,' said Father, and he chuckled. 'Fearfully pleasant cove, Winston. Reminds me of an ablutions wallah I once had in Goa.

'Or was it Madras? I don't suppose it really matters.

'In my experience bowel movements are the same the world over.'

And William chuckled, too.

He gave a sharp tweak to his sinuses and he said:

'I like Winston, I do. I really like him.

'He taught me how to French kiss.'

I bet he did, too.

Winston is an expert on all matters pertaining to amatory ventures.

15

I should know. I remember that day he and I . . . Never mind about that.

Dear Winston – poacher, gentleman, romantic, poet and out-and-out rogue and villain.

You don't find them like that at tennis club hops in the best part of Cheshire, I can tell you. What you get at tennis club hops in the best part of Cheshire are men who fumble at the straps of your bra and smell of stale beer and Lambert and Butler Straight Cut cigarettes when they kiss you in the groundsman's hut.

Dear Winston. When we moved into the village Winston transformed our lives.

He installed a new central heating boiler for us. He gave us a new stench pipe. Free and gratis. He got rid of the smell in the downstairs loo and introduced us to the works of Kingsley Amis.

And on the day of the village fete he took me into the woods at the back of his house, and we lay side by side at the foot of a great beech tree and he took off my blouse and we . . . we . . .

Yes, well never mind about that.

That's another story.

Once more the army helicopter roared low over the house and once more Father said:

'I say, helicopters. Fearfully pleasant brutes, helicopters.

'I wonder how many ladies the chaps have seen with no togs on. I once saw a lady with no togs on in Karachi. She had an exceedingly hooked nose I seem to remember.'

I felt the snarl deep in Rosie's soul as she said icily:

'Yes, Father, yes. We've heard all about it. Many times. For Christ's sake, we've heard it times without bloody number.'

'There's no need to shout like that,' said William grumpily.

'I'm not shouting.'

'You are.'

'I'm not. I'm not.'

As I said, we are indeed a happy, happy family. We keep ourselves to ourselves. We have very little to do with the life of the village. Winterleaf Gunner itself is gorgeous, of course.

It's the people who live in it who are so odious.

All those bumpkins with their smokers' coughs and their wrinkled stockings and their fat waddling bottoms and their gormless grins and their untidy gardens and their vicious dogs with mottled gums and their hideous children festooned in snots and old birds' nests.

Why do people like that find it necessary to breed?

I know it does wonders for the manufacturers of dartboards and iron lungs. I know Woolworth's and the Tank Regiment could hardly exist without them, but for the rest of us they make life scarcely bearable.

And the wife-swapping brigade at the top end of the village is not much better.

You'd think vets would have enough on their hands castrating horses and sticking their hands up cows' bottoms without turning their attentions to their neighbours' wives.

The front door bell rang.

No one moved.

'Is someone going to answer that bell?' I said.

There was no response.

'I see. Do it yourself, Nancy. As usual. As always.'

I put away my crocheting and went to the door. I opened it, and there stood Winston.

Winston with his lime-green woolly hat jammed low over his forehead and his long black hair curling over his shoulders. Winston with his wellies flapping round his ankles and covered in slime.

Winston with his shirt open to the waist and the tattoos above each nipple.

Over the right the word 'Mild'.

Over the left the word 'Bitter'.

I looked at him, and my heart turned over and melted.

It really did, even though he stank to high heaven of rancid sardines and there was a bluebottle buzzing round his navel.

4

'Whatho, Nancy,' said Winston. 'What do you reckon then? Not a lot.'

I smiled at him and said:

'Hullo, Winston. Isn't it a simply lovely day?'

'To be sure he is, missus. Without a doubt. Well, it always is a lovely day in autumn, ain't it? Particularly when old Winston's in the company of a handsome, beautiful woman in the prime of her life with a snow-white lissom neck and her berdongers all rampant.'

'We'll leave my berdongers out of this, Winston, if you don't mind.'

Actually I have to confess that my berdongers – my breasts, I should say – were looking particularly choice that evening. I've always been rather proud of them. I was easily the first to have any at school.

Muriel Wakefield was furious. She drew a rude picture on the blackboard and got gated for a week. Serve her right, I say.

I wonder what's happened to her? If there's any justice in the world, she'll be living in Basingstoke with a deaf aid.

'Don't stare at me like that, Winston,' I said. 'You know I hate being stared at.'

'I ain't staring, Nancy,' said Winston. 'I'm thinking.'

'What about?'

'The walk what I just done on the way to your house. I come by the river bank look, and I seen the old kingfisher plopping into the water and the old mink with the grey muzzle skulking in the reeds and the old barn owl hunting low over the water meadows and the larks singing their bleeding heads off.'

'How lovely.'

'Yes,' said Winston. 'I wish I'd brought my gun with me.'

'Winston! What a dreadful thing to say.'

He chuckled and the folds of his nut-brown belly wobbled and his shoulders shook and dislodged tiny specks of dandruff which twirled away lightly in the soft evening breeze.

Then he winked, tapped the side of his nose slyly and said:

'It's the ways and the wiles of the country, missus. You're not living in the city now look. You're living in the country, my dear.'

'I'm quite well aware of that, Winston, thank you very much,' I said tartly. 'Now then, what can I do for you?'

He shuffled his feet on the gravel and a shifty look came to his eyes.

The sun was beginning to sink behind the great banks of beeches and the towers and turrets of Florey Palace. We went there once or twice to take tea with the Duke of Wiltshire. Father still potters down there occasionally, but I don't. I couldn't stand the Duke ogling my berdongers and . . . my breasts, I should say.

I looked back to Winston and he was still shuffling his feet and he was rattling the loose change in his pocket.

'Well, come on, man,' I said. 'Spit it out.'

He coughed. He spat and wiped his mouth with the back of his hand and then he said:

'Well, Nancy, it's like this. I been thrown out of my house.'

'What?' I said.

'The missus have gone and turfed me out lock, stock and barrel.'

'What?'

'The missus, Nancy. You knows her. She's the ugly old party with the big backside and the droopy tits.'

'What?'

'I wish you wouldn't keep saying "What?", Nancy. It's perfectly simple look. My missus have objected – took umbrage look – to my bits of fluff.'

'Your bits of fluff?'

He smirked and speckles of pride glowed in his eyes.

He chuckled and said:

'My bits of fluff, Nancy. The women I has on the side look. Everyone knows about old Winston's bits of fluff. You ask Rosie. Ask yourself,

Nancy. Think of the day of the village fete when we went into that wood at the back of my house and . . .'

'Thank you, Winston, thank you very much,' I said. 'I don't think we'll go into that, if you don't mind.'

Once again he chuckled and the folds of the nut-brown belly he'd run over my thighs wobbled, and beads of moisture came to the lips he'd roved over my nipples.

'Cor blimey Charlie,' he said. 'That old beech tree – he could tell you a thing or two about my bits of fluff, if he'd a mind to.'

'Winston! That's enough.'

'Right, Nancy, right,' he said. 'You don't mind if I scratches myself in a personal place, do you?'

'I'd rather you didn't,' I said.

But he did. And it was a very personal place indeed.

I shivered. Dusk was beginning to fall and I was feeling cold.

I didn't want to let him in the house. Well, I'd got a pan of damson chutney on slow simmer and I didn't want Winston dropping bits off his navel into it. It was bad enough last year with the Christmas pudding. Father nearly choked to death on one of his toenails.

So I turned to him and said briskly like I used to do at the school debating society:

'Right then, Winston, let's get this straight. Your wife has thrown you out of your house because she objects to your infidelities.'

'In a manner of speaking, Nancy,' he said. 'It's like *Madame Bovary* only in reverse look.'

'I don't understand, Winston.'

'It's simple, Nancy,' he said with a smile. 'My missus have at long last took the hump on account of my constant and never-ending galli-vanting and have got herself a blokey.'

'A blokey?'

'Yes. Gilbert Spurfield from the ironmongers. He moved in last night with his stamp collection and his hover mower.'

He smiled again and nodded.

He looked so happy, so contented. I felt a flush coming to the side of my neck and my heart began to pump.

'Well, I don't know what to say, Winston,' I said and I had to cough to stop my voice from cracking. 'I mean . . . I mean have you thought what you're going to do? Have you made any plans?'

'Yes,' he said.

'What?'

'I'm going to move in here with you.'

'What?' I said. 'What?'

I couldn't believe my ears. My legs began to tremble. I went hot. And then I went cold. A tawny owl hooted and Winston kept staring at me with a great booming grin on his face.

I put my hand to my throat and said:

'What did you say, Winston? Tell me again. I think I might have got it wrong.'

'No you hasn't, Nancy,' he said. 'Not you. You never gets things wrong, does you; my old wingsy bash?'

And he put his arm round my shoulder and drew me into him. And I didn't resist. I just melted into his body.

He began to stroke my hair and then he said:

'It's the best thing all round, Nancy. Couldn't have worked out better look. I comes to live with you, and you've got me constantly on hand, ain't you?

'I'll keep my eye on your stench pipe. I'll wait on at table. I'll drive you round in my motor, my car look. I'll do all your repairs and renovations, drain your septic tank, unblock your drains and your guttering and explain to you in simple terms the philosophy of Jean-Jacques Rousseau and his *Social Contract*.'

I tried to speak. But I couldn't. He pulled me closer into him and he whispered:

'Right then, Nancy. It's all settled then. My gear's in my motor, my car look. So I'll just go and fetch Eric.'

I wrenched myself away from him and cried out:

'Eric? Who's Eric?'

He smiled his great booming smile again and said:

'He's my dog, Nancy. He's a lurcher. You'll like old Eric. You'll love him. He's shit hot when it comes to catching rats.'

And so Winston moved in.

And so did Eric.

5

Eric was indeed shit hot at catching rats.

Every morning he brought them into the kitchen for inspection. He left them in Rosie's studio and William's study. He left them in the drawing room under the display cabinet. He buried one in Father's bed and next morning Father came down to breakfast with the brute in his hand and said:

'Did I ever tell you about the time your mother and I were in Karachi and had fricassee of rat for supper?'

Eric had other talents, too.

One morning when we were sitting in the drawing room taking a break for elevenses, William burst in and shouted at the top of his voice:

'That dog. That bloody dog! Do you know what he's done now?'

Rosie looked up from her book – *The Social Contract* by Jean-Jacques Whatshisname – and said:

'Keep your voice down, William. Don't get hysterical.'

I thought William's eyes were going to pop out of his head. His face turned scarlet and his mail-order executive ball bearings clattered furiously in the pocket of his oatmeal cardigan.

'I am not getting hysterical,' he shouted in that high-pitched, weedy little voice of his. 'I am keeping very calm. My brain is precise and icy with concentration as I tell you dispassionately and coolly that that bloody dog has eaten chapter one of my new history of the Great Eastern Railway.'

'Oh dear, William,' I said. 'Can't you sort of . . . well, can't you change it to the Great Western Railway?'

Honestly, I thought he was going to explode and make a mess on the Chinese rug or what was left of it after Eric's predations.

'No I cannot change it,' he screamed. 'I have spent the past ten months of my life in the most meticulous research into every aspect of the finances, operating methods and rolling stock policies of the Great Eastern Railway.

'Then last week – last week at long last – I was prepared to start. The creative sap was in full flow. Every nerve end tingled with artistic anticipation. The words just flew and soared. And then this morning – what happened this morning? I'll tell you. I come into my study to discover that that bloody dog has eaten the first chapter and all my notes on the swing bridge at Beccles.'

At this Father put down his book – *Gimlet Mops Up* by Captain W. E. Thingie – and said:

'I once had a dog rather like that in India. Fearful brute he was. He ate the steering wheel of our neighbour's Frazer Nash tourer.

'Or was it a Wolsley convertible?'

Honestly, I thought sparks were going to shoot out of William's bottom and he'd go soaring through the ceiling like one of those rockets that always failed to go off when we were children.

He puffed and he panted as he struggled to control himself.

And then at length he said in a strangled voice as though his underpants were too tight:

'Who cares what make the car was, Father? All I care about is that Winston and that dog are destroying the whole fabric of our life and . . . and . . .'

He broke off, slumped into the small boudoir chair Mother had won at golf in Dunoon all those years ago and said softly:

'Oh dear. Oh dearie dearie me.'

I wanted to take him in my arms and cuddle him. I would have done, too, only I was frightened his ball bearings would damage my whatsits.

So I just smiled and said:

'Yes, William, it is a bit of a mess, isn't it?'

'Well, you've only yourself to blame, Nancy,' said Rosie icily. 'You're the one who invited him to stay.'

'I did not invite Winston to stay, Rosie,' I said. 'He invited himself. He just barged past me with his cardboard boxes and his black plastic bags bursting at the seams and now he's . . .'

'And now's keeping me awake all night snoring his head off and whistling through his teeth in the spare bedroom,' said William, and I swear he was almost sobbing.

Father tapped out his pipe into the plate of Garibaldi biscuits and said:

'Well, bung him in the shed then.'

'What?' said William.

'Bung him in the shed at the bottom of the garden. That's what we did with blighters like him in India. The shed at the bottom of the garden was always full of them – little brown buggers crouched up in their underpants and staring at their big toenails.'

'Father,' I said. 'Oh, Father. Not now. Please, not now.'

Rosie stood up and strode purposefully to the french doors. She stood there for a moment looking out over the garden and then she turned and said:

'There's only one thing for it – we'll have to hold a family conference.'

Father slapped his hands with delight and showered his plus fours with a cascade of red-hot tobacco fragments.

'A family conference? I say – how splendid,' he said. 'I love family conferences. Fearfully interesting. If I should fall asleep, there's no need to bother waking me up.'

And so that evening after dinner we held a family conference. We didn't draw the curtains in the sitting room. We let the stars crackle at the window panes. We let the moon grin at us.

William was dressed in his oatmeal cardigan, cavalry twill trousers and a check shirt with his official LNER stationmaster's tie.

Rosie wore her lovely emerald-green kimono and her blonde hair was held at the nape with a black velvet ribbon. She looked gorgeous. I could have eaten her, but I was frightened her diamanté dragon brooch would get stuck in my earrings. Things like that are always happening to me.

Father was wearing bus conductor's trousers, a white linen jacket and a navy-blue silk shirt with canary-yellow tie. He was bare-footed in his open-toed sandals. Aren't old men's feet dreadful? I think they should be banned.

And as for me – well, who cares what I was wearing?

Suffice it to say that if I'd been a spectator at the Boat Race, I just know the Cambridge cox wouldn't have been able to keep his hands off me. Filthy little swine. Why can't he pick on someone his own size?

Usually I like family conferences. I'm very good at them. I let everyone have his or her say and then I have my say and everyone does as they're told. I do like neatness and tidiness in human affairs, don't you?

But that night I just couldn't arouse any interest.

My mind kept wandering to Winston.

What was he doing? Was he using my toenail clippers again to trim his moustache? Was he sticking his gilberts on the corner of the oilcloth on the kitchen table? Was he happy? Was he out with one of his bits of fluff with yellow teeth and big berdongers? Was he trying to make it up with his wife, his missus? Did he want to go back to her? Was he tired of living with us? Did he like being in the same house as me? Did he like smelling my perfume when I'd been to the loo? Was he fed up with my cheery laugh and the butter under my fingernails when I made french toast for Father? Oh Lord, was he happy? Really, really?

He'd done nothing about the house since he moved in. Not once had I seen him paying attention to the stench pipe. Indeed he seemed to go positively out of his way to ignore it. He hadn't served at table or unblocked the drains. Not once had he rewired the house or put a new roof on the stables. All he'd done was hose down his dog in the bathroom and hang his dirty socks over the bannisters. Oh Lord, was he happy? Really, really?

At length Rosie stood up and said:

'Well, someone's got to start this bloody conference, I suppose.'

'Certainly, Rosie,' said Father. 'Fire away, old bean. Don't pay attention to me. I'm only your father.'

Rosie glared at him. She's the best glarer I've ever met in the whole of my life. If they had a Nobel Prize for Glaring, she'd win it hands down. The moon sickled the glow of her golden hair as she faced us and said:

'Well, the way I look at it is this – Winston is now firmly established in this house and . . .'

'And his dog,' said William. 'Don't forget that bloody dog.'

Rosie scowled.

'All right, all right – pedant,' she said. 'Winston and his dog are now firmly established in this house. Now then, do we want things to stay that way, or do we want to change them? And if so, how do we go about doing it? Do we reason with him? Do we threaten him?'

'We could always shoot him,' said Father.

'What?' said Rosie.

'Or we could get one of those helicopter chappies to take him up in his machine and drop him out over the mushroom farm.'

'He'd bounce,' said William.

'What?' said Father.

'He'd bounce right back up into the helicopter with a great triumphant grin on his face, and then he'd try to sell the pilot the services of his disgusting second cousin from Yeovil Junction. At special discount price, too.'

Rosie's eyes flashed. Oh, how they flashed.

'Don't be so idiotic, the two of you,' she said. 'Let's try and be sensible and cool and calm and collected for a change, shall we?

'Let's each one of us in turn give our opinion about whether Winston should stay or whether he should go. Right then, Nancy, over to you.'

I almost jumped out of my skin.

'What?' I said. 'What's that you say?'

'You've not been listening, have you?' said Rosie with one of her snarls. 'You've not heard a word I've said.'

'I'm sorry, Rosie. I'm sorry. How rude of me,' I said. 'It's just that I'm . . . I'm . . . all those memories. It's so strange. They've just come flooding back.'

To my intense surprise Rosie's mood softened and there was warmth in her voice when she said:

'What memories, Nancy?'

'Memories of our last house in London,' I said.

'Ah yes, I remember that,' said Father, slucking at his pipe and shaking the droplets from the stem on to the Chinese rug. 'Fearfully pleasant place, our last house in London. It had those exquisite wrought iron balconies and a wonderful view out over the harbour with the fishing boats bobbing and . . .'

'That was Scarborough, Father,' snapped Rosie. 'And for pete's sake, don't interrupt.'

She turned to me and smiled.

What a lovely smile she had, when she put her mind to it.

'Go on, Nancy,' she said softly. 'Go on.'

'I was thinking about the house spider,' I said. 'The day we moved from London he disappeared. I wonder if the new people have looked after him. I wonder if he's happy.'

'I expect he is, Nancy,' said Rosie. 'Spiders don't look the miserable sort to me.'

They don't, do they? I've never seen a miserable spider in the whole of my life. Woodlice never look happy with their lot. Neither do wasps, if it comes to that.

I smiled and said:

'And after the house spider I got to thinking about the day we moved in here and the gas leak and the poor old boiler being condemned and looking so wretched about it.

'And we sat here in the cold on packing cases with night lights because all the fuses had blown. And then Winston came round with his lovely smile and the nicotine stains in the palms of his hands.

'And one day I looked out of my bedroom window, and there he was straddled across the roof ripping off the slates with his funny hammer, and he was singing at the top of his voice, and he was wearing the most ghastly luminous pink socks covered in rabbit tods, and he looked so happy.

'I'd never seen anyone look so happy. I didn't know people could look so happy. I'm a mature woman, and I didn't realize people could look happy without feeling guilty.'

William rattled his ball bearings and said:

'Yes, Nancy, yes. It's all very well going sentimental on us, but what we need now is the practical approach.

'I detest Winston's socks just as much as you do, but the manner in which he clads his feet is not the issue at stake, is it?

'What we've got to decide is our attitude towards his presence in our house.'

The prig! The unutterable prig. You'd have thought they would have knocked that out of him in the Boy Scouts when he won his badge for fretwork, wouldn't you?

Suddenly Father said:

'Can I smell burning?'

'What?' I said.

'I can smell burning, old boy.'

Rosie strode across to him and shouted:

'It's you, Father. You've set fire to your shirt-tail with your pipe. Stay where you are, and I'll put you out.'

She beat at him with a cushion and he sat in his chair chuckling placidly as acrid smoke rose about his shoulders.

When Rosie had finished, he sighed deeply and said:

'Do you know, chaps, it amazes me that the boffins haven't considered inventing a fireproof shirt for the use of inveterate pipe smokers.'

At this William could contain himself no longer and he shrieked in his pathetic little reedy voice:

'Will you please shut up and listen to me?'

'Certainly, old chap, certainly,' said Father. 'Keep your wool on. He's just like your mother, you know, only he doesn't play golf with bad grace.'

Rosie settled him in his chair with a smile and turned to William and said:

'Right then, William, as you feel so deeply and passionately about things, the floor is all yours. Be intensely practical and tell the meeting what you think about Winston.'

William gave a little snicker of triumph – pathetic little prat, and that's not being as rude as I could – and said:

'Well, I'll put my cards straight on the table and say that I like the chap. I think he's a good sort.

'Since we've lived in this village he's been absolutely invaluable to us. No – more than that. He's been essential. Without Winston I don't think we could have survived. I know he tends to pong a bit in the summer, but his loyalty to us has never been in question.

'Despite his tattoos, he's been a real brick.'

'I rather like his tattoos,' I said. 'I think they're fun.'

'So do I, old boy,' said Father. 'Gin and tonic – fearfully amusing words to have tattooed above one's nipples.

'Did I ever tell you about that nude woman with no togs I met in Karachi and . . . Sorry, William, old chap, you were saying?'

'I was about to say, Father, that I look on Winston as a personal friend. A close friend. A very close friend indeed who has always been unfailingly kind and generous to me.

'It's just that . . . just that . . .'

'Just that what, William?' snapped Rosie.

I saw William squirm. He clenched his fists deep into the pockets of his oatmeal cardigan. He ground his teeth and screwed up his eyes.

And he blurted it out.

'He can't stay here. He can't live with us in this house.'

'Why not, William?' said Rosie, and there was a chill behind the calmness in her voice.

'Because he's not our sort,' said William, half-mumbling and rubbing his ankles together.

'Why isn't he our sort, William?'

'Good grief, Rosie, it's obvious.'

'Not to me.'

'Of course it is. You know perfectly well that he's uncouth and vulgar and . . . and . . .'

'Common?' said Rosie.

William's face lit up and he said with a smile:

'Common, Rosie. Exactly. Winston might be the salt of the earth. He might have a heart of gold. But deep down, basically, he is irredeemably common.

'He is not our sort.'

'What a disgustingly snobbish thing to say.'

'It's not.'

'It is, William. It bloody well is. You don't understand the first thing about Winston, do you?'

'Don't I indeed?' said William, and there was the faintest hint of a challenge in his whingey little voice.

I waited for Rosie to blow her top, but her voice remained calm.

'No, William,' she said. 'You know nothing about Winston. Okay, so he slurps his soup. Okay, he takes his shoes off in the dining room and sniffs his socks. Okay, he leaves his pubic hairs all over the bath mat.

'But all that is just superficial. It doesn't mean a thing. Winston is a

29

gentleman. He's cultured. He's sensitive. He's loving and intelligent. He's witty. He's the most superb company, attentive and polite and courteous.

'You don't know these things. You've never been out for an evening with him in his motor, his car.'

'Of course I haven't, Rosie,' said William, and he snickered smugly. 'I'm not one of his bits of fluff, am I?'

'How dare you say that.'

'It's true. It's true.'

'It is not true.'

'It is. It is.'

And so they started. And, oh my gosh and my golly, did they get stuck into each other.

Rosie's face went red and her eyes came out on stalks. William ground his teeth again and rattled his Great Western Railway commemorative cufflinks. And I looked and I thought – a happy family?

Us a happy family?

Don't make me laugh, boyos.

We are the most quarrelsome, argumentative family I have ever met in the whole of my life. We can't do anything together without the most monster disputes and rows.

Why? What's wrong with us?

I go into the garden with Rosie to look at the flowers, and we quarrel.

William asks Rosie to help fit a new ribbon on his typewriter and five minutes later they're in the middle of a blazing row. We try to do something warm and generous and supremely happy like planning a special treat for Father's birthday and we end up ranting and raving at each other.

Why?

Why do we suspect happiness so much?

Why do we hate it and fear it?

Why can't we be like Winston – simple, direct, totally gluttonous for happiness?

Winston! Dear old Winston, so full of love and mischief. Winston, so gentle, so warm, so . . .

'Nancy, Nancy.'

It was Rosie. Her hair had snatched itself free from the velvet ribbon at her nape, and the long golden tresses flowed over her shoulders and down her back. She looked stunning. If she'd have been a spectator at the Boat Race that nauseating little Cambridge cox with the pink transparent eyes and the sickly quiff would have . . .

'Yes?' I said. 'What do you want?'

'It's your turn now.'

'What?'

'William's had his say about Winston. And so have I. Father's fast asleep so he doesn't count.

'Right then. No hiding. No skulking. Come out into the open and tell us whether you think Winston should stay or whether he should go.'

And, do you know, before I could stop it I heard myself saying:

'He should go.'

'What?' said Rosie, and she stepped back a pace or two and the colour drained from her face.

'It's quite out of the question for him to stay here,' I heard myself say.

'Why, Nancy? Why?'

I tried to stop myself. But I couldn't. The words came pouring out like water flooding through a broken sewer, like golloping slurry spewing down a broken-backed hillside. I couldn't keep them back.

'Winston doesn't fit in,' I said. 'He doesn't belong here. He's dirty. He's smelly. His manners are appalling. He's rude. He's disrespectful. He's lazy and boorish and brutish and . . .'

And at that moment the door was thrown open and Winston entered.

I could not believe what I saw.

The stubble had disappeared from his chin. His hair was neatly cut and sleeked back with pomade.

And he was wearing a black alpaca jacket, pin-striped trousers and patent leather dancing pumps.

And over his left arm he carried a stiff, starched, snow-white napkin.

And he bowed deeply and said:

'Supper is served.

'Oh yes, that it is without a doubt.'

6

We were speechless.

We didn't move.

He bowed again. He turned and pulled into the room a trolley Mother had brought back from Fort William all those years ago.

On it was laid our best dinner service with the silver cutlery Mother had won in the golf tournament at Sandwich all those years ago.

And the whole trolley was groaning with food. Literally.

And it looked delicious.

And it smelt divine.

It looked absolutely, ravishingly, exquisitely scrumptious.

Winston smiled faintly and then he said:

'Just a little something I knocked up look.'

Still we didn't speak. Still we didn't move. He busied himself round the trolley, shaking out napkins, removing the lids off tureens and sticking his thumbs in the gravy boats.

And then he spoke again.

'Right then,' he said. 'I'll tell you what everything is just so's you knows what you're supposed to be eating.

'If you'd like to wake up your old dad, Rosie, I shall now commence and begin.'

Rosie woke Father gently. He opened one eye slowly, but when he caught sight of the trolley, he sat bolt upright in his chair and said:

'I say – grub. Whacko. Jolly Dee. Yum, yum, yum.'

Winston nodded gravely to him and then began to move slowly round the trolley.

'Right then,' he said. 'You has a choice of starters. Pickled salmon, canapés à la créme or a nice fricassee of eggs.

'For your joint you got roast pork with pistachio nuts or you might like to try the chicken liver with grapes provided you got a strong stomach and you don't mind getting pips stuck on the roof of your mouth.

'Now then, for the vegetables you has a choice of asparagus with new potatoes, savoury cucumber and a chilled haricot bean salad.

'For your dessert you has the option of gooseberry flan or a selection of French cheeses freshly garnered from Poole Harbour this very morning.

'Well, don't sit there looking all gormless with your mouths wide open like a nestful of constipated pelicans.

'Get stuck in and enjoy yourselves. And I don't mind if you has a good fart when you've finished look.'

And so we got stuck in. Oh yes, did we get stuck into that meal. And it was superb. It was gorgeous. It was delicate, refined and infinitely subtle.

'Winston,' said Rosie. 'These canapés are absolutely delicious.'

'So's the pickled salmon,' said William. 'Wonderful.'

Winston bowed and clicked his heels.

'Thank you,' he said. 'Now then, would you like your claret now or would you prefer to wait till I brings the glasses in?

'There wasn't no room on the trolley, see. Mind you, if you're gasping you can always have a few swift slugs straight from the bottle, can't you?'

'I think we'll wait till you bring the glasses in, Winston, if you don't mind,' I said. 'Crumbs, this pork – magnificent.'

'Thank you, Nancy. Much obliged,' said Winston gravely. 'You know what the secret of it is? You know why he looks so good on your plate?'

'No,' I said. 'Tell me.'

'You soaks him in saltpetre for a good three days and you makes sure the dog don't sniff him with his nose or cock his leg on him.'

'I say,' said Father. 'That's a fearfully interesting tip I must say. I like getting tips. I once got a tip from an air-raid warden in Grangeover-Sands. Can't for the life of me remember what it was. Those bloody gas masks, you see. I was always getting my thumbs trapped in the side, and the Perspex always got steamed up at the front and . . . I say – asparagus. Jolly Dee.'

We ate on. On and on and on. We gorged ourselves. Shamelessly. Our chins glistened. Our fingers ran with sauce and gravy. Our jaws ached. Our palates crooned.

And not for one second did we quarrel.

And when we had finished the meal and sunk back into our chairs, exhausted and replete, I swear there was the faintest, softest whiff of happiness in the air.

And I hardly dared to breathe lest it skulked away all hang-dog and forlorn and guilty.

'Right then,' said Winston. 'You seem to have finished look. I do hope the meal was to your satisfaction and your liking, and I shall now clear away the debris and return of an instant and in a trice with the port and brandy – I thank you.'

And then he bowed again and clicked his heels and said:

'Cor blimey Charlie, what a load of bleeding gannets you are without a doubt.'

He wheeled the trolley out of the room with a stately flourish. We didn't look at each other. We didn't speak. Our eyes were wide open with wonder. Father sucked up the gravy from the bottom of his canary-yellow tie.

Then Winston returned with the silver tray Mother had won at bridge in Inverness all those years ago and served brandy to the women and port to the men.

Was that right? I didn't think it could be. I'm sure Soames Forsyte or whatever he called himself would have disapproved.

And then Rosie spoke.

'Winston. Winston Hayballs, that was the most delicious meal I have had for years,' she said. 'It was just wondrous, my darling, lovely man.'

And she went up to him and hugged him and kissed him full on the lips.

Winston bowed impassively and said:

'Thank you, Rosie. And I hope you won't be kept up with it all during the night.'

William went up to him and shook him warmly by the hand.

'Where on earth did you learn to cook like that, Winston?' he said.

'From books, William.'

'Books?'

'From books, William. Same as I learned everything in my life,' said Winston gravely. 'That's how I discovered my wife was as ugly as sin look.'

'How, Winston?' I said. 'How?'

'Simple, missus. I was reading this book by the poet. Alexander Pope sort of thing, and he was writing about some bint what had got the vapours.

'Well, I wasn't much interested in that look. I'd had enough trouble with the fumes from the exhaust of my motor, my car look. No, what interested me was the way old Alexander Pope described her. He built up this real genuine picture sort of thing, and I could see her as clear as if she was sat next to me in the outside bogs – all long silky blonde hair, snow-white skin, long smooth neck. He didn't say nothing about her berdongers look, but, by God, she didn't half sound tasty to me.

'And then I looked up from my book, and there was the missus sat opposite me smiling with her mottled arms and eating a satsuma with her legs wide open.

'Dear oh dear, I thought to myself. If they hung you for being beautiful, you'd die an innocent woman.

'Yes, that's how I realized that my missus was really, really ugly.'

I felt so proud of him. God knows why, but he looked so handsome, so manly, so masterful. He looked so happy, so proud, so contented. He looked so subservient. I think subservience looks very manly in a man, don't you?

He turned to the door and said:

'Well then, if you're all satisfied and well-serviced, I shall retire, leave you and depart. I bid you goodnight.'

'Wait a minute, Winston,' I said. 'There's just one thing before you go.'

'Yes, Nancy?' he said.

'Where did you get all this food from?'

He smiled and tapped the side of his nose.

'Ah, missus, ah. That would be telling,' he said. 'That it would without a doubt.'

'You didn't steal it, did you, Winston?'

'No, Rosie. It's swapsies.'

'Whatsies?'

'Swapsies, Rosie. All swapsies. You'll be amazed what you can get in the country with forty-six pounds of salmon poached fresh from the river with nothing but two metal coat hangers and half a stick of dynamite.'

William coughed nervously and said:

'I rather wish you hadn't told me that, Winston.'

'Oh, don't you bother your arse about that, William,' said Winston. 'I rather fancy the local bobby's having grayling for his supper tonight look.'

He bowed again and made for the door.

Then he paused, turned and said:

'Oh yes. Before I goes I got something to tell you.'

'And what is that, Winston?' I said in the voice Mother used to use on the point duty policeman in Knutsford all those years ago.

'Well, Nancy, it's just to say that I have put a new ribbon on William's typewriter, repaired all the locks on his filing cabinets and changed the stylus on his radiogram sort of thing.'

'I say,' said William. 'It takes me three weeks to put a new ribbon on my typewriter. Thanks a million, Winston. You're a real brick.'

'You're very welcome, William,' said Winston, and then he turned to Rosie and me and bowed.

'And as for you two ladies – well, I've washed and ironed all the bedding, I've got you a brand new freezer second hand sort of thing from unnamed sources, and I've put your knickers to soak in fabric softener in a bucket in the utility room.

'Oh yes, and when your old dad wakes up, you can tell him I've mended that hole in the backside arse of his plus fours.'

A smile came to his face. The stiffness and propriety of his composure vanished. He winked at us and said:

'Right then, I'll be away. The sight of all this food and drink have got my gastric juices racing something chronic. So I'll be off to the pub for a swift sesh look and a packet of pork scratchings.

'And who knows, eh – there might even be a bit of fluff in the offing.'

He strode purposefully out of the room and slammed the door behind him.

We were silent for ages and ages, and then Rosie said:

'Well then?'

'Well then indeed,' said William.

'So what have you to say about Winston now, William?'

The muscles in William's jaws began to twitch. He hitched up his socks. He pulled them down again and began to scratch his shins. And then he looked up, smiled and said:

'Well, I don't suppose the swing bridge at Beccles is all that important really.'

Rosie smiled her lovely, glowing smile and said:

'And you, Nancy? What have you got to say.'

Well, there was only one thing to say. And I said:

'Me?' I said. 'I think I had one helping too much of the gooseberry flan.'

7

I slept soundly that night.

I didn't have a hint of tummy trouble.

Of course I wanted Winston to stay all along. Of course I did. There wasn't the slightest doubt in my mind about it.

At the family conference I was playing the part of the devil's advocate. Of course I was. Not the slightest doubt about it.

It was a simple matter of practicalities. Of course it was.

In Winston we had our own resident odd-jobman, cook, chauffeur, home decorator, gardener and philosopher. Most people would give their hind teeth for a man like that about the house. No doubt about it.

And that's the only reason why I consented to allow him to remain. It was. It really was.

Without a shadow of a doubt sort of thing.

When I got up next morning, I found Winston hard at work planting herb cuttings in the kitchen garden.

I stood behind him silently.

The sun beat down.

He was naked to the waist.

I think every house should have an odd-jobman with broad shoulders, rippling arms and a nut-brown belly, don't you?

I coughed softly. He turned round and smiled.

'Whatho, missus. What do you reckon then? Not a lot,' he said.

I breathed in deeply and said:

'What a lovely smell, Winston.'

'Yes, you can't beat the smell of rosemary, Nancy,' he said. 'If you ever has an hangover from drinking stale beer, just stick a sprig of rosemary up your schonk piece and you'll be as right as rain in time for the pubs when they opens at dinnertime.'

'Thank you, Winston,' I said. 'I'll bear that in mind.'

'Oh, there's plenty I could teach you about herbs, missus. See this borage here?'

'Yes,' I said.

'Well, if you ever gets a nanny goat with an infected udder look, all you got to do is . . .'

'Winston.'

'Yes, Nancy?'

'I want you to tell me something.'

'Fire away, my old wingsy bash.'

'Well, what I want to know, Winston, is why you cooked that superb and stunning meal for us last night.'

He chuckled deeply. It was a lovely chuckle like the noise water makes twirling through the plughole when you've had a long, long soaking hot bath.

He tapped the side of his nose, winked and said:

'Just give me half a mo with this fennel, Nancy, and I'll take you a walk along the river bank and tell you about it.'

It was a beautiful morning. The river sparkled. We saw the kingfisher. We crossed the single plank of the wooden bridge, and Winston held my hand. The leaves sighed and rustled contentedly on the Cuckoo Tree. Bullocks stood silent and fetlock deep in the shallow waters of the ford.

Voles rustled.

'Let's sit down on the bank by this old pool, Nancy,' said Winston.

'All right,' I said.

We sat down side by side on the bank. Winston unbuttoned his shirt and stuck his right forefinger deep into his navel. Then he extracted it and sniffed at it.

I wanted to scream. But I didn't.

If you employ a live-in knicker-washer and part-time philosopher, you have to learn how to put up with behaviour like that and always conduct yourself in a ladylike manner. Just look at the Queen at the Trooping of the Colour.

He sighed deeply and said:

'This pool, Nancy, he's the finest pool on the whole stretch of the river. Many's the prime salmon and succulent brown trout I caught in here. Oh yes. Without a doubt.

'And many's the time I've come to swim in it totally bollock-naked apart from my old birthday suit.'

'When you were a little boy?' I said, stretching out my limbs and letting the preening sun linger over my body.

'No, no, missus,' said Winston. 'I'm talking about the present look. I often comes down here and has a good old splog around in the altogether. You wants to come with me and try it some time, Nancy.'

'Winston,' I said. 'What a dreadful thing to say.'

He chuckled again. He rolled himself a damp cigarette. He sucked in at it silkily and let the blue smoke dribble and coil over his lower lip.

Then he said:

'So you wants to know all about my plans and my motives, do you, Nancy?'

'Well, I must say I'm rather intrigued, Winston.'

Winston nodded, stubbed out the cigarette on the heel of his welling-ton, stuck it behind his ear and propelled a long silvery arc of spit into the river.

'The thing is, Nancy,' he said. 'The thing is I'm chuffed till Friday tea time that the missus have booted me out of the house sort of thing.'

'I rather gathered that, Winston.'

'Best thing that's happened to me since I got stuck in the lift with my cousin, Betty Hayballs, at Weston-super-Mare.'

'I don't think I want to know about that, if you don't mind, Winston.'

'No, Nancy. That you don't without a doubt,' he said.

He lay back on the springy river turf and gazed up into the clear blue sky.

'See, Nancy, see, when the missus booted me out of the house look, I thought to myself, I knows what I'll do. I'll go and live with the Empsons. I'll sling my hammock with old Nancy and Rosie and William and their old dad. They'll love having old Winston living with them. It'll be just the ticket.

'Am I right, Nancy? Is that what you thought?'

'Well, Winston ... well, we're very happy to help you out of a temporary hole,' I said. 'We're very happy indeed. I mean, we're only too delighted to rally round and give you a roof over your head while you sort things out for yourself. And I'm sure as soon as you have, you'll be wanting to move on.'

'But I has sorted things out, Nancy,' he said. 'That's what I'm trying to tell you. That's why I give you that meal last night look. That's why I'm doing all these jobs round the house for you.'

'I don't understand, Winston.'

'I'm doing it to lull them into a false sense of security.'

'What?'

'Listen, Nancy. What I does is this – I pampers them, see. I spoils them and cossets them. They thinks old Winston's the best thing since sliced bread. They sings his praises to the heavens. In their eyes he can do no wrong. And that's when I pounces, Nancy.'

'You pounces, Winston? What on earth are you talking about?'

'That's when I starts to sow the seeds, Nancy. A word here. A word there. A whisper. A rumour. A hint. And then I've got them in my hands like putty, Nancy.'

'You've got me completely lost, Winston.'

'No, I ain't, Nancy. It's simple look. I've got them all set and ready, ain't I? I've sowed the seeds in their heads that they got to leave the village, leave the house and move away into the great big wide world yonder.'

'What?'

'Rosie, William, your old dad. Oh, yes, Nancy, once old Winston's finished with them, they'll be off and away with a smile on their face, a spring to their step and then there'll be just you and me, Nancy.

'Just you and me together and alone.'

I felt the blood rushing to my head. I felt my temples pounding and my eardrums roaring.

'What the hell are you talking about, Winston?' I shouted. 'How dare you? How dare you talk to me like this? How dare you? You disgusting little man with your fat boozer's belly and your dirty front teeth – how dare you talk to me like that?'

And then I began to sob. I couldn't stop myself. The tears spurted out of my eyes and cascaded down my cheeks.

Winston did nothing.

He just propped himself up on one elbow and said gently:

'That's all right, Nancy. You have your little weep, my lovely. Old Winston don't mind look. He don't care. He knows that in your heart that's what you wants. You and me together, Nancy. Just you and me.

'Because, Nancy, I loves you. I desires you. I wants you.'

A jay cackled. A heron flapped hunched and leggy slowly over the ford. House martins twittered.

And then suddenly Winston jumped up and said: 'Right then, I'm going for a swim, Nancy. Want to join me, do you?'

And with that he tore off all his clothes and plunged into the pool.

And he splashed and he shouted, he wallowed and he guffawed. He turned turtle and dived. He floated on his back. He blew out great founts of water from his mouth and all the time he was laughing.

And do you know – for a moment I almost felt like joining him.

But only in my imagination sort of thing.

8

Three days later Winston shot Eric.

Just like that.

Bang! And he was dead.

This is how it happened.

It was a simply gorgeous morning. The sort of morning that makes you want to dash out and buy up the whole of Harrods' soft furnishing department.

The walls of my bedroom glowed with autumn. They feasted off it. They crooned to it. They were sated with it.

I sat at my dressing table grooming my hair with the inlaid tortoise-shell brushes Mother had won at golf in Portmanock all those years ago.

I felt so happy.

Me. Nancy. Happy. What on earth was going on in the family?

We'd hardly had a tantrum worth the name out of Rosie. William pottered about the house all day in his brown gym pumps with the pimpled toecaps singing to himself and trying to be helpful with the Venetian blinds. And Father gluttoned back his food like a battalion of the Black Watch and never once forgot to pull the chain after he'd used the lavatory.

Ever since we told Winston he could stay on in the house our lives had been engulfed by happiness. There was no getting away from it. It bounded up at us from dark corners. It trilled to us in the swooping eaves. It rocked us gently in our beds and whispered in our loins and all our cool and secret places.

I looked at myself in the mirror.

Was I really desirable? Did someone really love me and want my body?

Was it possible that I could bring happiness to another human being?

Then I heard the screams.

'Nancy! Nancy! Nancy!'

It was Rosie. And she was hysterical.

'Nancy! Nancy! Nancy!'

I rammed my head through the collar of my mauve-and-cream striped jumper and dashed downstairs.

I found Rosie in the garden. She was standing there rigid. Her elbows were drawn tight to her breasts and her hands were clasped tightly round her ears.

'Nancy. Oh, Nancy,' she sobbed.

At her feet was a rabbit. It had no head.

'Oh, my God – Eric,' I said softly to myself.

And then I shouted at the top of my voice:

'Winston! Winston, come here this instant.'

And from the kitchen he called back:

'Right you are, Nancy, my old wingsy bash. I'll just bung my Provençal pine-nut gateau into the oven and I'll be with you in a jiff.'

And he was indeed with us in a jiff – the village poacher, nut-brown belly as ripe as the autumn, and the tattoos above his nipples and the drooping Zapata moustache and the stubble on his chin and the blue-chipped gap between his two front teeth.

I pointed at the dead rabbit with my foot.

'Winston,' I said. 'Remove it.'

'Certainly, missus,' he said with a smile and a wink.

And he picked up the rabbit and stuffed it into his shirt.

'Oh Christ,' said Rosie, and she heaved.

Oh my gosh and oh my golly how she heaved.

At this I saw red. I really did. My blood was boiling. I was livid.

'Winston,' I said. 'Remove that rabbit from my sight.'

'Yes, missus,' he said.

'And, Winston.'

'Yes, missus?'

'Remove Eric. At once.'

'Yes, missus.'

He sauntered off, chuckling to himself and slapping the side of his wellies with a switch he'd snapped off the clematis.

I took Rosie into my arms. She shivered. I stroked her lovely long golden hair and ran my lips softly over the rims of her ears.

And then.

Bang!

Just like that. Bang!

Rosie stiffened. And then she tore herself from my arms and fled into the house sobbing.

I positively flew down the garden. And there at the bottom next to the compost heap I found Winston. He was placidly scratching his crutch and smoking a straggly cigarette and at his feet lay the body of Eric.

'Winston,' I cried. 'For God's sake, man, what have you done?'

'Removed Eric,' he said. 'I done what you said, missus. I shot him look sort of thing.'

I felt I was going to faint. I felt I was going to collapse. I struggled to speak.

'But . . . but . . . but when I told you to remove Eric, I didn't mean you to . . . I didn't think for one minute you'd . . .'

Like I had done to Rosie only seconds before he took me in his arms and began to stroke my hair. I didn't resist. I didn't yield to him, but I didn't try to draw away as he talked softly to me.

'It's the best way, Nancy,' he said. 'That old dog, he loved me, see. Well, I couldn't give him to no one else, could I? He'd have pined away and died, wouldn't he? That's what happens when you loves someone, Nancy. You sends them away from you, you don't have nothing to do with them and life ain't worth living for them no more, is it?'

He held me tightly to him.

He held me tightly for ages and ages and I felt the calm and steady beat of his heart and smelled the tobacco in his stubble and the scent of pine nuts in his hair.

At length he whispered to me:

'So you won't ever think no more about sending old Winston away, will you, Nancy? Cos if you did, I don't know what he might do with himself. That I do not. Without a shadow of a doubt.'

45

9

'Isn't it strange how quickly you forget about dogs?' said William. 'One minute they're there. Next minute they've gone and you can't remember for the life of you who it was used to eat up the scraps after we'd finished supper.'

'Yes,' I said.

And I thought to myself – I wonder if it'll be like that when Father dies.

We were sitting on the patio after dinner.

The summer bats were still flittering their funny flitters and an army helicopter clattered fitfully in the distance.

Father looked up from his pipe and said:

'Do you think this Winston chappie will be staying here long, Rosie?'

'I don't know, Father,' said Rosie. 'Why do you ask?'

'Well, it's just that he reminds me of this Indian wallah I knew when I lived in Chittagong with your mother when she was alive. Or was it Lahore? I don't suppose it matters all that much really.'

'Get on with it,' snapped Rosie. 'I haven't got all day, you know.'

'Ah, but I have, Rosie, I have,' said Father. 'That's what makes life so fearfully beastly at times.'

Rosie's eyes softened. She leaned forward, patted Father gently on his knees and said:

'I'm sorry, Father. Come on and tell me all about this Indian wallah you knew in Chittagong or was it Lahore?'

Father scraped at the bottom of the bowl of his pipe with one of our best fruit knives and said:

'Well, we moved into this house, your mother and I, and it was completely empty except for this Indian chappie sitting in a corner in the kitchen. He was a plump little cove with a moustache curved down over his mouth like a damp sickle.

'He smiled at us, and we smiled back.

'We didn't know who he was. Neither did our neighbours. Neither did our servants.

'He just sat there in the corner smiling at us. And when we left, he was still there.

'I expect he's still there now smiling and scratching his crutch.

'Just like Winston, don't you think?'

'Oh yes, Father – just like Winston,' I said.

Winston! What was he doing? He'd given us a scrumptious dinner. He'd ironed my underslips immaculately. He'd washed Rosie's emerald-green kimono by hand and it hadn't shrunk an inch.

Winston! I thought about our walk along the river bank and how we'd sat by a pool and a heron had flapped slowly overhead trailing his lazy legs and a green woodpecker had yaffled and cackled and Winston had told me of his plans to get rid of Rosie and William and Father and we would live alone together here in the old Dower House.

And the more I thought about it, the more appalled I was.

I was horrified. I was outraged.

He wanted to form an attachment with me. Me a mature, educated, sophisticated woman.

I'd been to private grammar school. I'd been to Florence. Three times. I'd eaten Toblerone in Switzerland when sweets were still on ration here. I'd been up the Eiffel Tower and had afternoon tea in Fortnum and Mason's. Not at the same time, of course, but my world, my whole background was completely different from Winston's.

What did I want with that disgusting village poacher with his fat, brown belly smeared with grease and old cow pats and his beastly tattoos above his nipples and his dirty thumbnails as big as advertising hoardings and his flapping wellington boots and his . . . and his . . .

And yet.

And yet, and yet.

Something had to be done.

I put down my sewing and set off in search of Winston.

I found him in the stables sawing a length of wood.

'What are you doing, Winston?' I said.

He turned and smiled at me.

'I'm making a cabinet for Rosie, missus,' he said.

'A cabinet?'

'That's right, Nancy,' he said, dousing the stub of his cigarette on the tip of his tongue. 'Well, you knows all them fabrics sort of thing what she designs? Well, she's got to have somewhere to store them proper, so I'm making a cabinet for her. Yes. I'm making it from that old yew tree what I nicked from the Palace grounds the winter before last. Designed it myself, I done. Shit hot, eh?'

'That's enough, Winston,' I said. 'That's quite enough of that language, if you don't mind.'

There was a naked bulb burning brightly and swaying by a flex thrown over a beam. There was a smell of varnish and sweet wood shavings. There was a row of chisels laid out neatly on a bench. A half empty bottle of home-made country wine stood askew on the floor propped against a fat, stunted log.

Winston took off his woolly hat, scratched at his gritty hair and smiled again. He whistled through the gap in his teeth and said:

'Cor blimey Charlie, I don't half fancy you, Nancy, when you has your dander up.

'Your eyes, they flashes away something chronic and your berdongers, they heaves and they bucks and they bounces, and you looks bold and you looks handsome.

'You looks terrible tasty, Nancy. Terrible tasty without a doubt.'

I was not to be trifled with. I was not to be soft-soaped.

I took firm control of my berdongers, my breasts look, and I said sharply:

'Winston!'

'Yes, Nancy?'

'Winston, what are you doing about your wife?'

'My wife, Nancy?'

'Your wife, Winston. Your missus. Have you made any effort to see her since you've been here?'

'No,' said Winston.

He picked up the bottle of wine and glugged at it greedily.

Then he smacked his lips, smiled and said:

'Well, why should I, Nancy? She's as ugly as sin, my missus.'

'But what about your children?'

'The ankle-biters? What about them?'

I'd once had half a day's training for the Samaritans, so I knew I was on firm ground when I said:

'Winston, it might have escaped your notice, but to my certain knowledge on the last count you had at least nine children.'

'That's right, Nancy,' said Winston, taking another swig of his wine. 'Nine sprogs, and all as ugly as their mother. Can't stand the sight of them, I can't, and that's a fact sort of thing.'

I pursued my theme with my best telephone voice.

'That might well be the case, Winston,' I said, 'but the point is that you have a duty and an obligation to support them. Not only financially, but emotionally. It's your bounden duty to see them regularly and write them letters and . . . why are you staring at me like that?'

'Cos you're a beautiful woman, Nancy. You're no spring chicken, that I knows without a doubt, but you are beautiful, my old wingsy bash.

'You got nice ankles. Slim. You got nice legs. Long. You got a good bosom, too, missus. Yes. He's all firm and succulent, is your old bosom.'

'Winston. Please. I . . . I . . .'

I felt a flush coming to the side of my neck. I felt my knees trembling and my cheeks quivering.

Winston finished off his bottle and tossed it on to a pile of damp sacking in a shadow-flickering corner.

He stared at me silently for a moment, and then he said:

'You thought anything more about what I said to you on the river bank by the pool the other day?'

Ah. Now I was on safe ground once more. I was mistress of my emotions. I was fully in charge of myself.

I straightened my shoulders, hardened my lips and said:

'As a matter of fact I have, Winston, and that is precisely why I am here.

'I want to make it perfectly plain and categoric that I . . .'

'You leave it all to old Winston, Nancy,' said Winston softly. 'The silver tongue. The honeyed tongue. That'll make them go, Nancy. Rosie, William, your old dad – sweet as a nut they'll go. Then it'll be just you and me, Nancy. On our own. On our tod.'

He was so firm. He was so secure. He was so sure of himself. What could I say?

I flustered. I fumbled.

'But don't you see, Winston?' I said. 'Don't you understand? The whole thing is quite preposterous. It's ludicrous. It's . . . it's . . .'

I began to sob again. Just like I did on the river bank where the jay cackled and the green woodpecker yaffled.

'Oh, Winston,' I snuffled. 'Oh, Winston, Winston.'

But this time he did not put his arms around me.

He just stood there, stroking the tips of his moustache and sucking in softly through the gap in his two front teeth.

'That's right, Nancy. Have your little sob,' he said. 'You looks lovely when you sobs. Without a doubt you does.

'You leave it all to old Winston, my lovely. It'll all work out in the end. Things always does, when you leaves them to old Winston look.'

What on earth was going on?

Once I used to be miserable.

How lovely it had been.

10

Nancy Empson, unmarried, long-legged, bold and handsome, firm-breasted and in her mid-forties spent the whole of the following morning in her sewing room.

She locked the door and did not stir.

In the sitting room William, Rosie and Father were gathered to take elevenses.

The sun still shone.

Rosie wore a navy-blue fisherman's smock and jeans, and Father wore plus fours and an I Zingari cricket sweater with singe marks on the hem.

William took a bite from his fig roll and said:

'I'm worried about Nancy.'

'Really?' said Rosie. 'Why?'

'Because she's behaving rather strangely.'

Father stirred his beaker of hot chocolate with a pipe cleaner and said:

'It's the time of the year, old boy.'

'What?' said William.

'Spinster ladies of a certain unmentionable age and condition always behave in a curious manner when the wasps bumble at the necks of jars of sticky jam and the sap withers in the trunks of gnarled old apple trees and the summer's abdominal protector is tucked up snugly in its winter wrappings.

'I remember this spinster lady in Udaipur. Or was it Benares? I don't suppose it matters all that much really. The point is that she had this bald parakeet, and every time the monsoons came, she . . .

'Sorry, Rosie. You were saying?'

'I wasn't saying anything,' said Rosie gently. 'I was trying to ask William why he thinks Nancy is acting strangely.'

'It's her attitude to Winston,' said William.

'Winston?'

'Yes,' said William, dunking the remains of his fig roll in his caffeine-free coffee. 'Why hasn't she thrown him out of the house? Nancy is always throwing people out of the house. She threw my cub mistress out of the house when we lived in Bridgenorth. She threw your badminton partner out of the house when we lived in Boston, Lincs.

'Why hasn't she thrown Winston out of the house?'

'Oh, William, it's very simple, my sweet,' said Rosie. 'Winston has a way with him. Winston weaves his spells. And we're all under the sway of his magic. None of us can escape it.'

She finished her camomile tea and savoury rice cakes and returned to her studio.

She had not been there for more than five minutes when the door opened and Winston stepped in.

'Hello, Rosie,' he said. 'Not disturbing you, am I?'

'Not really.'

'What are you doing, if I may be so bold as to ask and inquire look?'

'Oh, it's just a doodle, Winston,' said Rosie. 'I sent off some designs to a fashion house in London, and as soon as I posted them I knew they were a load of rubbish.'

Winston sucked through his teeth and nodded sombrely.

Rosie smiled at him.

'So I'm doodling, Winston,' she said. 'I'm trying to find a new voice for myself. Do you understand?'

'I thinks I does, Rosie. It's sort of like when you decides you needs to choose a new flight for your darts, ain't it, sort of thing?'

Rosie nodded and he continued:

'I likes what you're doing, Rosie.'

'Do you, Winston?'

'Oh yes, without a doubt. They got nice patterns them designs. Nice colours, too. All different. Very tasty. Very handsome.'

Then he paused and rubbed the stubble on his chin thoughtfully.

'Rosie,' he said.

'Yes, Winston?'

'Well, I was thinking, conjecturing sort of thing, about whether you would like to come out with me tonight sort of thing in my motor, my car look.'

Rosie beamed broadly and said:

'Winston, I'd love to. What a smashing idea.'

And she gave him a swift peck on his left cheek.

I peeked above the curtains in the window of my sewing room and watched them leave the house in Winston's motor, his car.

Rosie's blonde hair glowed and sparkled and shimmered. She was wearing a scanty white linen top with bare arms and a long wide floral skirt which flowed and rippled.

And she looked absolutely terrific.

And Winston!

He looked terrific, too.

He was wearing a navy-blue corduroy suit. And it was very well cut. He was wearing a pink shirt. And that was very well cut, too.

And he had a yellow cravat with red fox heads on it. And it was beautifully knotted.

His hair was slick and neatly combed. The stubble on his chin had been shaved away. And he had the look of a man who smells of expensive gents' toiletries.

Oh, yes, he looked really really terrific.

What was he up to?

What the hell was he up to and where was he taking her?

The answer was simple.

Winston was taking Rosie to a public house in Gridley Miskin high on the hills above Crannock Chase.

As Nancy Empson crept upstairs to her bedroom so as not to disturb her father and her brother he conducted Rosie into the concert room at the rear of the sad-eyed pub with the drooping lintels.

He sat her down at a table under the Hunt calendar and the fixture list for the point-to-point.

On a platform at the far end of the room a jazz band chuntered and chunnered. The trombonist had home-knitted maroon socks and a Bakelite hearing aid.

'Do you like it here, Rosie?' said Winston.

'It's very nice, Winston,' said Rosie. 'Pity about the band, though.'

Winston nodded and said:

'Yes, well, it's better than them space invader machines and one-armed bandits, ain't it? Nowhere near as musical, is it?'

Rosie smiled. 'No, I don't suppose it is.'

Winston grunted a greeting to Lionel Woodyates, the postman from Winterleaf Gunner with the permanent thread of spittle between his lips, then he moved his chair closer to Rosie and said:

'Rosie? Are you happy, Rosie?'

'Pardon?'

'Are you happy with your life?' he said urgently. 'Are you happy living in the country? Are you happy living in that house with your old dad, your spinster sister, your bachelor brother and your defective stench pipe?'

'I think I am, Winston.'

'You don't sound sure.'

'Don't I?'

'No.'

'Why do you ask? Why do you look so concerned?'

Winston moved even closer to Rosie and said:

'You're a beautiful young woman, Rosie. Very tasty.'

'I think you're quite tasty, too, Winston.'

'I know,' said Winston. 'That's what all my bits of fluff says.'

'And modest with it, too.'

'Oh yes, Rosie, that I am without a doubt. I'm bleeding famous for my modesty, I am.'

He scowled at Nansen Ticehurst and his son, Peary, from Winterleaf Gunner who had just delivered a load of logs to the landlord of the pub.

Then he took hold of Rosie's hand, squeezed it tightly and, after looking rapidly over his shoulders, said:

'Have you ever thought about going back to London?'

'What?'

'London, Rosie. That's where you belongs.'

'Is it?'

'Course it is, Rosie. You knows that as well as what I does. You knows it better look.'

'Do I, Winston?'

'Yes, yes, without a shadow of a doubt.'

He went to the bar and returned with a gin and tonic for Rosie and a pint of scrumpy and a whisky chaser for himself.

'You knows them designs what you draw, Rosie?' he said.

'Yes.'

'Well, in my capacity as a fervent admirer and cognoscenti look of the works of Cézanne, Van Gogh and the shamefully neglected Gustave Caillebotte, 1848 to 1894, I thinks they're bloody good.'

'Thank you, Winston.'

'So under them circumstances, Rosie, what you wants to do is this – you wants to go back to London and draw them there.'

'Why?'

'To be near your customers, see. That's the secret of making a living, Rosie. Be near your customers. Be near your raw materials.

'I'm a poacher look. Well, it'd be no good to me living in London, would it? Would it buggery. You ain't got deer and pheasants and grayling and geese from old Mrs Fokine's backyard in London, has you?

'If I had to rely on poaching them in London, I'd be flat broke and going to exhibitions at the Tate Gallery with my do-dahs hanging out of my breeches backside, wouldn't I?'

'Yes, Winston, I suppose you would.'

'That's why I lives here. Near to my customers. Near to my raw materials. And that's why you should live in London.'

Rosie smiled, patted Winston on the knee and held up her empty glass for a refill.

They were plotting. They were hatching things up. I could feel it in my bones.

I tossed and I turned in my bed.

I used to do that when Mother was out at the golf club and Father was downstairs drinking gin and falling over the occasional coffee tables.

I used to twitch and itch at dead of night when the house was silent and the landing seemed to be prowling with loneliness and the cups on the hooks of the Welsh dresser drooped with sadness.

People were plotting.

People were plotting against me.

Me. Good old Nancy.

But what were they plotting?

When Winston returned to the table with the drinks, he put his arm round Rosie's shoulders and said:

'You live in London, Rosie, and you'll find yourself a blokey as quick as a collie pup catches worms.'

'What?'

'I know you've got me now, and I'm all handsome and desirable look, but the thing is I'm already spoken for in a manner of speaking sort of thing.'

'I see, Winston.'

'So with me out of circulation what chance have you got round here of finding yourself a blokey concomitant to your great beauty and your dazzling talents? Sweet bugger all, my old wingsy bash.

'Oh, I knows there's a case could be made out for Desmond Saltmarsh from the bicycle shop, but you mustn't let yourself be carried away by him, Rosie.'

'No?'

'No, I knows all my bits of fluff thinks he's well-endowed and always gives them a discount on their saddle bags. But there's more to a long-term partner than that, ain't there, Rosie?'

'Yes, Winston, I suppose there is.'

The jazz band slouched off for their interval drinks and Lionel Woodyates took his teeth out and picked them clean with a brass peg from the crib board.

Winston stared long and deep into Rosie's eyes and continued.

'That's why you got to turn your mind to London, Rosie,' he said. 'You think of all them eligible, desirable young men going begging there.

'They always got clean collars look. They never smells of cowshit or breaks wind in public. They got manners, see, Rosie. And they got fast

56

motors, fast cars, and swanky flats with them baths with taps at the side so's you don't have to lean forwards and expose your arse to the cold.

'They'd take you out, Rosie. Give you a good time sort of thing. You'd go to the races at Sandown Park and you'd have a picnic out of the back of their Rolls-Royce with pink champagne and clean serviettes.

'You'd go dancing at the Ritz with a cleavage. You'd go to galleries and museums. You'd go to the theatre and see plays wrote by proper authors.

'You'd be cosseted and cherished and have your toenails cut every week by people specially qualified to do it.'

'But that's not what I want out of my life, Winston,' said Rosie. 'I'm happy as I am.'

'Are you, Rosie? Are you sure?'

'Yes, I am.'

Winston looked furtively over his shoulders again. He poured the dregs of his whisky into his pint of scrumpy and he said earnestly:

'Are you sure you're happy living in that draughty old house with a draughty old spinster sister what bosses and bullies you and don't understand that you're a beautiful young woman and in a different league from her as regards the firmness of your berdongers?'

'Winston. Please.'

'Are you happy living with a bachelor brother what clucks under his teeth all day long like a broody old hen and writes them bloody stupid books about railways including points and signals?'

'Winston, Winston,' said Rosie, and there was a tremor in her voice.

'Are you happy living with an old father what talks on and on endlessly and forever about the experiences what he had when he lived in India? Or was it Burma?'

'India,' said Rosie. 'But I don't suppose it really matters.'

Winston stared at her more intently and he began to stroke her beneath her chin.

'That's no life for a lively, attractive, sensitive, intelligent, talented young woman like you, Rosie,' he said. 'Get yourself off to the big city. Get yourself a career. Get yourself a blokey.'

'I don't want a blokey, Winston. I'm happy as I am.'

'Are you, Rosie? Really, really happy?'

'Of course I am,' snapped Rosie, and she flared her nostrils and flashed her eyes.

But then her shoulders drooped and she bit her bottom lip and said: 'At least I think I am.'

11

Next evening Winston cooked us the most superb dinner.

French turnip soup, tripe fritters, gammon with apricot stuffing and brandy and greengage truffle.

It was delicious.

And he served us home-made elderberry wine with the main course and home-made gooseberry wine with the dessert.

And it was delicious.

All through the meal I watched him like a hawk, but he gave nothing away. His dress was formal, his manner correct and his conduct at table impeccable.

Once our eyes met. I raised my eyebrows ever so slightly, but he made no response. He stared rigidly ahead and did not once scratch his navel and sniff his finger.

At the end of the meal Father kicked his napkin under the table, tapped out his pipe in the pot pourri bowl and said:

'Whacko. Jolly Dee. Fearfully pleasant nosh, old boy. Fit for a maharajah. Heartiest congratters.'

'Thank you. Much obliged,' said Winston. 'And what about you, Rosie? Did you enjoy the meal?'

'What?' said Rosie vaguely.

And I snapped:

'Rosie! Winston's talking to you. What's the matter with you? You've not said a word all through dinner.'

'Haven't I?' she said. 'I suppose I must be thinking.'

'What about?' I snapped again, all my hackles rising and my toes scrunching up in the brogue flatties I bought in Winchester when things like that were fashionable.

'Oh, this and that, Nancy,' said Rosie. 'Picnics at Sandown Park. Baths with taps on the side.'

Winston chuckled and in an instant I knew what he was up to.

He'd made a pass at Rosie. That was it – he'd propositioned her. After all he'd said to me, after all the flattery and the fine words and the heavy breathing and the stroking of hair and the clasping of bodies flesh against flesh he'd . . .

Good God, he'd proposed marriage to her.

That was it. Of course it was. He told me once when he was ironing my panties that he always proposed to his bits of fluff when he took them out in his motor, his car.

Well, Rosie most certainly was not one of Winston's bits of fluff.

Just think of the family she came from. An uncle on her mother's side had received the MBE for services to the theatre organ. Her own father had once almost been seen in the company of von Ribbentrop. Her own sister had been to Florence three times and seen Alpine choughs from the window of the Jungfraujoch railway.

In no sense of the word was she one of Winston's bits of fluff.

If anyone in this household was Winston's bit of fluff, it was . . . it was . . .

I turned to Rosie furiously and I barked in my best Harrods' voice:

'Rosie, what on earth is the matter with you?'

She just smiled sweetly at me and Winston chuckled and said:

'Don't you bother your arse about it, Nancy. It'll all come out plain and simple in the end, that it will without a doubt.'

Then he turned to William and said:

'Ah, William. A word in your lughole, if I may.'

'Yes, Winston?' said William.

'I wonder if I could intrude on your reveries for a moment and discuss some matters with you pertaining to matters of a personal nature.'

'Yes, I suppose it's all right,' said William hesitantly. 'Fire away.'

'In private,' said Winston firmly. 'In your study, if you please. You can follow me there now.'

And to my astonishment William stood up and trotted off meekly out of the room after Winston.

What was going on? What was Winston up to?

What was Winston doing to us?

Nancy Empson, unmarried, brimming with love, weary with happiness, pinched by unfashionable flatties was not to know as she paced up and down the room while her father and her sister sat quietly by the piano playing bezique.

Meanwhile in his study William was confronted by Winston.

'Right then, William,' he said. 'I was wondering, surmising sort of thing, what book you are engaged upon in writing just now at this present moment in time?'

William looked startled. He jangled at his cufflinks and said:

'Well, as a matter of fact, I'm . . . are you sure you're really interested, Winston?'

'Me? Old Winston? A lifelong admirer of the works of Mrs Gaskell, Jean Rhys, Iris Murdoch and literary bints of a similar nature? Of course I'm bleeding interested.'

'Well, nobody else in the house is. Nobody takes the slightest interest in what I write. Never mind the fact that my books help pay for most of the running of the house. Never mind that . . .

'Why are you interested, Winston?'

'Because I ain't like no one else in this house, William,' said Winston. 'I ain't like no one in the world you ever met in your life, my old wingsy bash. So come on then. Tell old Winston what you're writing.'

William rocked up and down on his heels and smoothed down the front of his oatmeal cardigan and said:

'Well, just for the moment, Winston, I've abandoned my book on the history of the Great Eastern Railway. I don't seem to be in the mood. The inspiration isn't there. I've got stuck on the Ilford Carriage Sidings.'

'Well, you would, William. That you would.'

'So what I've done is this – I've gone back to a favourite project of mine, a slim volume on the Manchester, South Junction and Altrincham Railway. Well, what do you think?'

'Rubbish,' said Winston.

'What?'

'You don't want to be writing books like that, William. What you wants to be writing is mucky books.'

'Mucky books?'

'That's right, William. Mucky books about glamorous people sleeping with each other regardless when they didn't ought to and doing rude things in Hollywood.'

'But I've never been to Hollywood, Winston.'

'Precisely, William. And I bet you never been rude with a woman of the opposite gender neither, has you?'

'Well, I . . . I . . .'

'Listen to me, William, there's a great big world out there beyond the confines of the Ilford Carriage Sidings.

'There's adventures to be had. Mysteries to be probed. Wild, rampant women to be explored in dark and sensuous places.'

William coughed nervously and said:

'Yes, well, as a matter of fact I *had* thought of writing about women.'

'Yes?'

'Yes. I was going to write about their role as ticket collectors during the two world wars.'

'That's the ticket, William. You got it, my old wingsy bash. You got it perfect.

'What you does is this – you writes this book about women ticket collectors on the Somerset and Dorset Railway sort of thing and underneath their plain navy-blue fustian tunics look they're wearing sheer silk black knickers and shimmering silver suspenders sort of thing stretched taut across sumptuous acres of firm pink thighs.

'And when they gets home at nights, William, they paints their naked bodies in carmine and cerise, and they smokes fat Turkish cigarettes out of long ebony holders and they has hours and unbroken hours of carnal passion with the chief shunting foreman at Yeovil Junction.'

'Yes, well, that's not quite what I had in mind, Winston,' said William.

'Course you hadn't, William. How could you? You ain't never travelled, has you? You ain't never seen life. You're stuck away in this village and the only hint of carnal passion what you gets is a sight of Betty Hayballs' bloomers hanging out of the back of Norbert Honeysett's laundry van, ain't it?'

'Yes, well . . .'

'You got to travel, William. Travel the world. Have adventures. Have dangers and excitements sort of thing.

'You needs to sail the South Seas in a wind-whipped schooner look. Drink strong black coffee and cognac with the ladies of the night in Paris. Make love to the dusky ladies of Araby. Romp naked at midnight on beaches with buxom blondes all tawny-skinned and . . .

'Cor blimey Charlie, William, I'm getting myself going here. I'm getting all worked up, that I am without a doubt.'

'Well, I'm not,' said William. 'I don't like that sort of thing. Strong black coffee gives me a headache, and I can't stand sand between my toes.

'No, Winston, I'm quite happy where I am, thank you very much. I love living in the country. I love living in this house. And I love writing my railway books.'

Winston smiled and patted him on the shoulder.

'That you does, William, without a doubt,' he said. 'But I tell you this – you'll never get fame and fortune writing books about railways, will you?'

'Fame and fortune?'

'Fame and fortune, William,' said Winston. 'You'd like that, wouldn't you?'

'Well, I don't know about fortune,' said William. 'But I have had a spot of fame in my time, you know.'

'Oh yes?'

'Certainly. For six years I was Hon. Treasurer of the Society of Railway Authors. I organized three successive trips to the loco sheds at Calais, and they were all voted an outstanding success even allowing for the sea sickness.'

'No, William, no,' said Winston. 'I'm talking about real fame and fortune. You write mucky books look, and you'll be rolling in money. It'll come tumbling out of your ears. It'll be clanking in your pockets as you drives through Mayfair in your chauffeur-driven Bentley Continental with the automatic ashtrays. It'll buy you anything you wants in life, William – fast cars, fast women, the whole panoply of the jet-set life with unlimited access to clean socks and rampant berdongers.'

'I've told you, Winston. I'm happy as I am. For heaven's sake, man, I'm happy.'

Winston picked up a paperknife from William's desk and began to burrow in his right ear. He picked up a blue HB pencil with a rubber at the end and used it to prod into his nostrils.

He winked, tapped the side of his nose and said:

'But what about esteem, William? Now esteem is something you'd really like, ain't it?'

'I have got esteem, Winston. I've loads of it. I'm extremely well-regarded among aficionados of the railway book genre. I get letters. Fan letters. Only last week I had a letter from a gentleman in Frodsham inquiring about . . .'

'I means real, genuine, authentic esteem, William,' said Winston. 'Long articles about you in the Sunday colour magazines with photos of you sitting in a hammock drinking chilled champagne opposite an advert for Swedish kitchens. Transatlantic flights across the Atlantic by aeroplane sitting next to a Hollywood actress what keeps licking your ankles while you're trying to open your packet of processed cheese with your gold propelling pencil.

'Instant recognition, my old wingsy bash.

'You walk down the Rue de Rivoli in Paris and all them Frogs are nudging each other and saying: "Cor blimey Charlie, *sacré bleu*, there goes old William Empson."

'You'd like that, wouldn't you, William? That'd make you happy.

'Really, really happy.'

William smashed his fist hard on top of his dove-grey filing cabinet and said:

'But I am happy, Winston. I tell you I'm happy. I am. I am.'

And then he paused, his shoulders drooped and he said weakly:

'At least I think I am.'

12

What on earth was going on?

What was Winston doing to them?

I was a mature woman with certificates in Domestic Science and a parchment scroll for crossing the Arctic Circle on an expensive cruise to the North Cape, and yet I was completely stumped.

For days Rosie walked round with a wistful look on her face and daydreamed throughout her meals.

She didn't lose her temper once.

She was nice to be with. She was pleasant company.

What had Winston done to her?

The autumn lumbered on like a great honey-golden bear with soft paws and a glistening muzzle stained with the juices of plump, perspiring berries.

And William?

William stopped writing. He jerked and twitched all day like he used to do before being sent to camp with the Boy Scouts. He rattled his cufflinks incessantly. He came out in a rash on his shins and his elbows. And one day I caught him shuffling bare-footed in a tray of sand I'd prepared for tomato cuttings in the greenhouse.

What on earth was going on?

And all the time Winston cooked us vast, delicious meals and washed and ironed, and hammered and sawed and drilled and hoovered and walked around all day long with a great smirk of contentment on his face.

And never once did he seek me out alone.

Never once did he try to take me in his arms and whisper into my ear and stroke my hair and pass flattering remarks about my long, lissom neck and the state of my berdongers.

Then one day I spotted him walking purposefully down the garden to Father's shed.

And he was carrying a brown plastic shopping bag.

Father! My God, he was turning his attentions to Father.

Nancy Empson dashed upstairs to the spare back bedroom but she could not see Winston knock on the door of her father's shed.

And she could not hear her father's answer:

'Come on in. It's only me.'

Winston opened the door and entered the shed.

'Hello there,' he said. 'What do you reckon then? Not a lot.'

'Ah, Winston,' said Father. 'Whacko. Jolly Dee. Fearfully nice to see you, old boy. Take a pew.'

'Ta very much,' said Winston, and he held up the plastic shopping bag. 'I brought you something. It's a present.'

'A present! I say. Stout fellow. Is it a surprise? Or can I open it?'

'Course you can open it. It's a bottle of gin.'

'A bottle of gin! My word, how splendid. Top hole. There's just one thing, though.'

'And what's that?'

Father chuckled.

'I don't drink gin,' he said. 'Well, not any more, I used to at one time. Oodles and oodles of it, old boy.

'I was a secret drinker, you see. Nancy didn't know, of course. Neither did Rosie nor William.

'That's the secret of being a secret drinker, you see – never let anyone catch you at it even though you know they know. A chap keeps up his self-respect that way, you see.'

'Oh yes, I sees that,' said Winston. 'Still, there ain't no harm in having a quick swig now, is there?'

'No. No, you can't tempt me, old boy,' said Father shaking his head firmly and averting his gaze from the bottle of gin Winston held before his nose. 'I've given up drinking for good and all, and I feel infinitely better for it. I can taste my food properly. I can smell the fresh-mown grass. My skin tingles. My blood runs pure. I've no aches and pains, no sticky tongue of a morning, no bile in the pit of my chest, no pains in my arms at the dead of night.

'And, my dear chap, it is absolute, unmitigated ghastliness.'

Winston unscrewed the top off the bottle of gin and said gently:

'Here you are then. Have a swig of this. You knows one of the greatest pleasures of stopping drinking?'

'No.'

'Starting off all over again.'

'Absolutely, old boy. Absolutely, old boy,' said Father.

He snatched the bottle of gin off Winston, cocked it to his lips and drank greedily from the neck.

He spluttered, he coughed, he fought for his breath. Then he put down the bottle and sighed deeply.

'Ah, that takes me back,' he said. 'Gin – the taste of India. Pink gin and clinking ice. A crescent moon, the howl of monkeys, the soft whirr of a sewing machine in the servants' quarters, the grunt of a tiger, the distant wail of the night express to Madras and oodles and oodles of gin.'

He took another swig from the bottle and Winston said softly:

'You liked India, didn't you?'

'Loved it, old boy. Adored it. The happiest years of my life were spent in India. I never wore a singlet once, you know.'

'No?'

'No,' said Father. 'I used to wear a boater. I had them specially made for me by this little knock-kneed blighter in Ahmedabad. Fearfully decent cove.'

'Yes?'

'Oh yes,' said Father golloping at another long draught of gin. 'I once went to visit him at his house. Can't think why, but I did.'

More gin. More coughing and spluttering.

He continued:

'He lived in this narrow, gaunt house with oodles and oodles of balconies. It was an excessively gaunt house and all the rooms were empty except for the one on the topmost storey. And in that room, old boy, lived the whole family. The man himself, his fat wife, his toothless mother, his six children and a goat.

'Frightful smell, old boy.

'The children stank abominably.'

'Well, they would,' said Winston. 'It's the same with ankle-biters the world over look.'

'Happy days,' said Father, supping at the gin once more. 'Happy, happy days.'

His eyes began to glaze and his chin began to nod at his chest.

'Have you ever thought of going back?' said Winston.

'Often, my dear chap. Often,' said Father. 'Oodles and oodles of times.'

'Then why don't you go?'

Father giggled. And then a serious mien came to his face and he said gravely:

'It's the legs, you see. The old pins.'

'You don't have to walk there, pillock,' said Winston, forcing another gulp of gin through Father's mouth. 'You goes by plane look.'

Father shook his head. He blinked hard three times. He wagged his forefinger aimlessly. Then he clenched his fists and said:

'I've only been on a plane once.

'A De Havilland Rapide.

'Rangoon it was.

'And there was a typhoon.

'A typhoon in Rangoon.

'Sounds lovely, doesn't it, old boy?

'A typhoon in Rangoon.

'A monsoon *and* a typhoon in Rangoon.

'A prune in Rangoon.'

He giggled, turned towards Winston blearily and said:

'Any more gin left, my dear old wingsy bash?'

'Without a doubt,' said Winston. 'You still has a good quarter of a bottle here look.'

Father took a long slow swig from the bottle and sighed.

'This is the life, eh?' he said. 'Oodles and oodles of . . . oodles and oodles of poodles eating noodles.'

He cackled with laughter and tried to raise the bottle to his mouth. He missed and struck his chin with its neck. He giggled again.

Winston, staring at him intently, said:

'Ain't you got a bit of money stashed away?'

'I should say so,' said Father. 'Oodles and oodles of money.'

'Well, what you wants to do is this – you wants to draw it out all nice and secret sort of thing and not tell a soul about it.

'Not Nancy. Not Rosie. Not William.

'And then what you wants to do is buy yourself an aeroplane ticket to India and fly yourself out there all secret so no one knows.'

Father struggled to keep his eyes open. He smacked his lips dryly. He tittered sleepily and said:

'I say, old boy. I say.'

Winston continued:

'And when you gets there what you does is you travels the whole length and breadth of the country, and when you've done that, you gets yourself a little house, a bungalow look, in the foothills of the Himalayas sort of thing, and you lives there with a slim, brown lady with dark, smouldering eyes and silver bangles on her ankles, and all you hears is the howl of monkeys, the grunt of tiger and the clink of ice in tumblers full of pink gin.'

'I say, old boy. I say,' said Father, and then his head fell forwards on to his saffron-yellow shirt and his sky-blue silk tie and he began to snore.

Tenderly Winston took the bottle of gin from his hands and downed it in a single gulp.

He looked down on the old man, and he said:

'You poor old bugger. You'll most likely snuff it before you ever gets through the duty-free at Heathrow Airport.'

A dewdrop quivered on the end of Father's nose and sparkled in the last rays of the dying sun.

13

And then Father started acting strangely.

He spent all morning in the shed at the bottom of his garden. And when he came out, his eyes would be sparkling, and he'd be giggling to himself.

And one day he asked Winston to drive him into town, and he came back with his old scuffed briefcase bulging and a large brass padlock attached to the handles.

And for the first time in years and years and years he stopped talking about India.

What was Winston doing to them?

What on earth was he doing?

I tackled him one morning in the kitchen when he was making a puree of aubergines and chestnuts and wearing the pinnie Mother had won at the whist drive in Llandudno all those years ago.

'What are you doing to us, Winston?' I said.

'Me, Nancy?' said Winston. 'I ain't doing nothing look. I'm being good old Winston as per usual. Good old Winston, attentive, generous, full of fun, full of love.'

He smiled, wiped his hands on his pinnie, tapped the side of his nose with his finger, winked and said:

'Full of love, Nancy.'

'Stop looking at me like that, Winston,' I said.

'It's only desire, Nancy. It's only lust.'

At this I screamed at him. Positively screamed at the top of my voice.

'How dare you use that word in my house. Don't ever let me hear you do it again. Do you hear me? Do you understand?'

He did nothing. He just smiled his long, slow smile, and in an instant all my rage subsided.

'Oh Winston, why don't you go?' I said. 'Why don't you leave us alone?'

'Because I'm here to make you happy, Nancy,' he said.

'But I am happy,' I said. 'We're all happy. We're deliriously happy. We never ever want to leave here. We never ever want things to change. We just want to be left alone. Leave us alone, Winston.

'Please, Winston.

'Please, please, leave us alone.'

And with that he took me in his arms and kissed me full on the lips.

I wanted him to go on doing it for ever. I wanted him to suck me gently into his mouth and I'd swim around there like a brightly painted tropical fish and I'd sleep there peacefully at night all calm and secure and I'd . . .

And then Rosie came bursting into the kitchen and shouted:

'They've accepted them. They've bought them.'

'Bought what?' I said, thrusting Winston away from me.

'They've bought my designs,' she said, clapping her hands together and planting a great kiss on Winston's cheek. 'The fashion house in London. And guess what, Nancy?'

'What?' I said.

'They've offered me a job there. They've offered me a job in London.'

Winston began to chuckle softly to himself.

And then Father and William came into the kitchen. They were talking animatedly. And they ignored me. They totally ignored me.

Father said:

'And I'll buy a little bungalow in the hills.'

And William said:

'And I'll buy myself a white silk suit with real turn-ups and I'll walk down the Rue de Rivoli and I'll be on television in Hollywood having my ankles licked.'

And Father said:

'And I'll drink oodles and oodles of gin and I'll throw the empty bottles at the monkeys and play bezique all night with a slim brown lady with dark, smouldering eyes and silver bangles on her ankles.'

And William said:

'And I'll be deliriously happy.'

And Father said:

'And so will I.'

And Winston chuckled.

And Rosie danced up and down.

And me? Good old Nancy?

I wanted to scream.

Very quietly. To myself.

As always.

As usual.

14

'Don't let that family of yours browbeat you and bully you, Rosie,' said Winston.

'Mm,' said Rosie.

'Don't let them blackmail you. Stand up to them. You been offered that job in London. Well, you take it.'

'Mm.'

'Show them two fingers and bugger off out of here pronto. You got to grab the chance to make a new life for yourself.'

'It's not as simple as that.'

'Why not?'

'Well . . . well, because they don't actually do or say anything I can get my teeth into. Do you understand that, Winston?'

'I thinks I does, Rosie.'

'It's the way they look at me. There's this deep pain and deep, deep hurt in their eyes. I feel like a traitor, as though I'm stabbing them in the back. And I just can't bear it. It's absolutely intolerable, the selfish bastards.'

'That's right, Rosie,' said Winston. 'Let it all come flooding out. All the bile. All the anger. You rest your head on old Winston's shoulder.

'Lovely, lovely, beautiful girl . . . you listen to old Winston, eh? And then you do as he says. There ain't no need to worry your pretty head just so long as you does exactly what Winston says sort of thing.'

*

Good God, he took her in his arms. He stroked the nape of her neck. And she closed her eyes and pressed herself into him.

What the hell was going on?

They'd been at it all morning in the garden.

I'd been watching them from behind the curtains in the drawing room. And they'd been laughing and whispering and touching each other's arms and holding hands and smiling.

And then he took her in his arms and . . .

I turned in to the room and said at the top of my voice:

'What the hell is going on?'

There was no response.

William sat hunched up on the piano stool like a circus chimpanzee scratching his ankles. And Father sat in the winged armchair by the fire fashioning spills out of the church magazine with all its misprints and toadying.

Trying to keep very calm – icy calm, in fact – I said in a soft voice:

'I'm talking about Rosie.'

'Oh her. There's no problem there, old boy,' said Father. 'I think she should go.'

'What?' said William.

'I think Rosie should take the job and go and live in London. Do her the world of good. Broaden her horizons. Put hairs on her chest and give her the chance to ride on trams and take afternoon tea at Lyons Corner House.'

'But what about me?' said William.

'What about you, William?' I said icily.

'If she goes, I'll be the only young person left in the house.'

'Well, I'm not exactly decrepit, you know, William,' I said. 'I've still got a good few years to go before I fall into my dotage.'

'I didn't mean it like that, Nancy,' said William. 'I know you're still young   in your own sort of way. You're in the prime and full maturity of being young. Good Lord, you've had years and years' experience of it.

'But the point is you are not as young as I am. And I need the stimulus of young people of my own age about me.'

'Why?' said Father.

'What?' said William, spinning round on the piano stool to face him.

Father smiled benignly and carefully stuffed the spills into the inside pocket of his green-and-red striped blazer with the moth-holed lapels and the hang-dog collar.

Then he said:

'You see, William, you're hardly a dashing young gadabout, old boy, are you? You're not my idea of the gay, abandoned, devil-may-care masher with a girl in every port and a chorus girl stashed away in a love nest in Sussex Gardens.

'What do you do with your life?

'You sit at home all day writing those ghastly books about railways and in the evening all you do is rattle your cufflinks.'

He smiled at William again and began to fill his pipe from the leather pouch Mother had brought back from Ventnor on the Isle of Wight all those years ago.

William jumped off the piano stool, and for a moment I thought he was going to attack him.

I prepared myself to kick him in the privates, but all he did was stand before Father, grinding his teeth, jangling his ball bearings in the pocket of his oatmeal cardigan and wobbling his silly little Adam's apple.

At length he spoke.

'How dare you talk to me like that?' he said. 'How dare you? My railway books are not ghastly. Everyone knows that I've given the world entirely new insights into the running of the Cheshire Lines Railway. Everyone knows that my history of the steam railways of the Low Countries is an absolute classic of its kind.

'And I do not rattle my cufflinks. I do not. I do not.'

'Calm down, William,' I said in my best Sea Ranger voice. 'Calm down. You'll come out in another of your rashes.'

'I do not come out in rashes,' said William. 'I am still a young man. And I'm telling you both here and now that it will be a disaster for me if Rosie leaves this house.'

'But why, William?' I said. 'You don't get on with her. You're always rowing and arguing.'

'That's only because we're extremely quarrelsome by nature.'

'Exactly, old boy,' said Father. 'You take after your mother there.'

'What?'

Father applied a lighted match to the bowl of his pipe and sucked in deeply. He coughed and the dense blue smoke coiled around him and floated away in filmy cloying layers to the french windows.

He rested his pipe in the saucer of his half-drunk beaker of consommé and said:

'Your mother, William, was the most quarrelsome woman I have ever met in the whole of my life. You'd say something simple and innocent to her like: "Hullo, old bean, nice day, isn't it?" And she'd bristle up and say: "What do you mean – nice day? It's a bloody awful day."

'So I'd say: "All right then, have it your way – old horse – it's a bloody awful day." And she'd say: "What do you mean? It's not all that bad."

'Yes, fearfully quarrelsome old party, your mother.'

Then he chuckled, turned to me and said:

'Nice day, isn't it?'

'What do you mean – nice day?' I said. 'It's a bloody awful day. Winston's out there in the garden cuddling my sister. The whole fabric of the family is cracking up in front of our eyes. Our lives are being ruined and all you can say is it's a nice day.'

'All right then, old boy, it's a perfectly bloody awful day,' he said in that relentlessly cheery manner which always made me wish I'd taken badges for throttling and disembowelling in the Sea Rangers. 'But I still think Rosie should go. I'd jigger off myself if I were thirty years younger.'

'What?' I said. 'What's that you say?'

'I said, Nancy, that I'd jigger off tomorrow, if I weren't so old and didn't enjoy Winston's cooking so much. I mean to say, old boy, it's hardly a stimulating life we lead here, is it?'

The alarm bells started to jangle. The sirens for Action Stations wailed and the gas warning rattles clattered.

'I beg your pardon, Father?' I said.

'Life's so boring here, Nancy,' said Father. 'It's mind-numbing. Frightful. I'm a widely travelled man. I've had adventures. I've seen the great natural wonders of the world – man-eating tigers stalking the swamps of the Sudan, Masai women smearing their bold and naked bodies with wild honey, Ranji scoring a ton before lunch at Maidstone.

'And look at me now – cowed, defeated, a prisoner of total, inexorable boredom.'

The maroons screeched up into the massing storm clouds, fizzing and fuming and lighting up the gnashing rocks and surf-spumed, crashing seas.

The sirens shrieked, the dive bomber tilted and commenced its howling plummet to the gentle moonlit cottage asleep in its soft, purple shadows – and the big guns opened up, tearing at the guts of the sky.

'Father,' I said. 'That is the most disgusting, obscene statement I have ever heard in the whole of my life. For the past twenty years this family has been total slaves to your whims and your caprices.

'We've travelled round the country, moving from house to house, from town to town, for one reason and one reason only – you.

'Why did we leave London to come here? Because of you and your sinuses? Or was it your dizzy spells or your fallen arches?

'Every place we've lived in we've just begun to settle in and make friends and complain about the milkman, and then we've had to move off again.

'Why?

'Because you couldn't manage the stairs. Or the public library brought on your cough. Or the neighbours' children brought on your catarrh.

'The whole family and its life has revolved round one person and one person only – you.

'And who has suffered most?

'One person and one person only – me.

'William's got his books. Rosie's got her designing. You've got your secret drinking.

'And what have I got?

'Nothing.

'I've dedicated my whole life to you. I've sacrificed everything. And now William turns round and tells me I'm an old maid. And you tell me I'm some sort of jailer locking you up in a prison of boredom.

'I hate you.

'I hate the whole lot of you.

'You've ruined my life.'

I stood there, panting and shivering and quivering at the knees.
And do you know what Father did?
He lit his pipe carefully, nodded to William and said:
'Mm. Yes. Bloody awful day, eh, William?'

15

It was true.

They'd destroyed my life.

Bastards.

Bloody autumn with its booming, boastful sun and its clamouring, jangling, irredeemably vulgar golds and russets.

Where was winter with its gales and its blizzards and its lumbering leaden skies and burst water pipes and chapped fingers and squelching slush and damp, clammy fogs and crashes on the motorways and floods in sodden valleys and funerals in graveyards creaking with frost?

I fled from the drawing room and locked myself in my bedroom.

I looked out of the window over the village.

The sun sparkled on the towers and turrets of Florey Palace. The smoke rose straight and still from the chimneys of the pantiled cottages.

Wrens chirred. Blue tits chirruped. Missel thrushes threw back their throats at the stinging blue sky. The garden robin curdled the deep-berried hollies with his creamy song.

Bastards – just wait till winter got them in its grip.

And what were they doing downstairs, my precious family?

Bastards – wait till I thought of another rude word for them.

Everything I'd ever done in my life had had only one motive – to keep the family together, to calm them down, to settle their quarrels, to foster their talents.

And what about my talents?

None. I hadn't even got the basic, fundamental talent of a woman – to find herself a man.

I'd been near it.

Many times.

There was the golf professional in the Dukeries. He was so attentive and kind. And he was terribly flattering about my work in the bunkers with a sand wedge. I got on really well with his wife's chow-chow until it bit me on the ankle.

Then there was that lovely radio producer in the West Country who lived next door to us with his lathe and wattle ceilings and his Morgan three-wheeler.

He used to wrinkle his nose when he laughed and he wore elastic-sided scuffed suede boots and pink fisherman's smocks.

I know he was keen on me.

He used to call me 'darling'.

But then he called everyone 'darling' – even the postman.

I think he might have asked me out to a dog show or something, if only he'd been more articulate.

And there was the professional tree surgeon from Bridlington and the environmental health inspector from the Manifold Valley and the . . .

So many men.

And each time just as we were getting closer Father stuck his oar in, and off we moved to another part of the country.

I was an attractive woman. I knew I was. I always had been. I was just as beautiful as Rosie only I was slightly older.

Well, what was wrong with being older than your younger sister? It was no crime, was it? It wasn't a cross you had to bear all your life.

So many men, and the one man who had stepped forward and come out into the open and made his intentions patently and perfectly clear was a village poacher.

Winston!

A beer-sodden philanderer with a fat brown belly and stubble all over his chin and tattoos above his nipples and . . . and . . .

Oh, Winston.

Oh, Winston, Winston, what were you up to, what spells were you weaving around us?

*

Downstairs in the kitchen below Nancy Empson's bedroom Winston was not weaving spells.

He was hard at work of a culinary nature.

The door opened softly and William stepped in.

'Not disturbing you, am I, Winston?' he said.

'Not really, William,' said Winston. 'I'm just in the middle of baking a Brabant praline torte with Kirsch sort of thing.'

'Oh,' said William. 'Is it a cake?'

'Oh, he's a cake, William. He's a cake without a shadow of a doubt, my old wingsy bash. And so you know what's in him and what his ingredients are?'

'No.'

'Then I'll tell you – braised pyjama cords, grated loofah, six ounces of engine drivers' snots and *demi glace* giraffe's toenails and all soaked in syrup of figs.'

'What?' said William.

Winston chuckled and patted him on the back with a flour-snowed hand.

'It's a joke, William. A joke designed to make you laugh, what is the purpose of all jokes of a comical nature look.'

He chuckled again.

'Now then, my old pile of stewed horse shit, and what can old Winston do for you?'

William hesitated for a moment and then he said:

'Well, you remember what we were talking about last week?'

'Yes,' said Winston. 'Betty Hayballs' natural endowments as regards her gynormous nellies.'

'No,' said William. 'About me changing my style of writing.'

'Ah yes, William. Writing mucky books instead of them railway whatsits with swing bridges and shunters' poles.'

'That's right. And you said if I wanted to do that, I'd have to leave here and roam the world and face all its dangers and excitements and have dark, wild adventures with wild, rampant women.'

'That's right, William. That I did.'

'Well, I was wondering what sort of clothes do you think I'll need?'

'What?'

'Well, I don't want to make a fool of myself, do I? I don't want to be improperly dressed when I'm drinking strong coffee and cognac with the ladies of the night in Paris.'

'Wait a minute, William, hold on,' said Winston. 'Do I gather, surmise like, that you have decided to take up my advice and sling your hook out of this house and the bosom of the family?'

'Well, not in so many words, Winston. But I was certainly considering it. It is quite high on my agenda for future projects after I've finished my slim column on the history of the Manchester, South Junction and Altrincham Railway.'

Winston smiled, took the top off a bottle of stout with his teeth, spat it into the bin with a clang and said:

'And what, William, if I might be so bold as to ask and inquire, has brought about this change of mind?'

'Rosie.'

'Ah, Rosie.'

'That's right, Winston. I've been awake night after night thinking about this job she's been offered in London and what would happen to me, if she took it. And I'm distraught, Winston. Totally distraught.'

'Well, you would be, William.'

'What would become of me?'

Winston took a long draught from the bottle of stout.

'I'll tell you, William, Old Winston'll put it fair and square to you sort of thing,' he said. 'You'd grow into a wizened little turnip of a man. You'd become a secret drinker like your old dad. You'd be slowly strangled by bitterness, slowly strangled by resentment and remorse for what you didn't do when you had the chance.

'And most likely your do-dahs would drop off, too.'

'Oh dear,' said William, timidly rattling at his cufflinks.

'Listen to me, William, you are facing the biggest decision in your life. The moment of crisis sort of thing. Make the wrong choice now, and your whole future will be blighted like a field of carrots over-whelmed by weevils and terminal vegetarian chinky rot.

'The choice is yours, William.

'The earth is being rent asunder under your feet.

'Stay where you are, and there's drudgery and despair. Leap across the divide, and there's fulfilment, excitement, artistic satisfaction and birds with towering great bristols sort of thing.'

He finished his stout with a flourish and hurled the empty bottle into the bin.

William shuffled his feet and tugged at the hem of his oatmeal cardigan.

Then he said:

'Oh dear. Oh dear, I think I'd better go and lie down for a minute. I knew that life was changing all around me this morning when I saw the postmistress wearing sun-glasses.

'Excuse me, Winston, I think I'm coming out in a rash on my elbows.

'Oh dear, oh dear.'

And he padded out of the kitchen, closing the door softly behind him.

Winston cackled and stuck both of his thumbs high into the air.

I turned away from the window of my bedroom and listened.

The whole house was full of voices.

The family was plotting against me. Every single one of them.

The walls were plotting against me, too.

And so was the bookcase in the drawing room and the Welsh dresser in the kitchen and the stench pipe and the central heating boiler and the manhole cover and that sweet little shellack button box in my sewing room that Mother had won at the Spelling Bee in Keswick all those years ago.

There was only one thing to do – hold an emergency family conference.

At once. That evening.

16

We convened in the drawing room that evening.

You might have noticed that sometimes I called it the sitting room.

Well, who the hell cares?

A room is a room is a room.

That's the way I felt that evening, anyway. If there had been a spare mortuary handy, I'd have leapt at it.

I stood at the french windows. There was a hint of rain in the air and the smoke from the damp-leafed fire in Mrs Fokine's garden was straggling and fluffing out its skirts.

Behind me I felt my family waiting for me to make the first move. Father was wearing his MCC spats, Rosie was wearing those silly Italian culottes that made her bottom look fat and podgy and William was wearing his commemorative LMS cufflinks.

I breathed in deeply, composed myself, turned and said:

'I've called this emergency family conference because I want to bring things out into the open.'

'What things?' said William.

'The crisis in the family.'

'Oh that,' said Father.

I turned on him with a snarl to my lips and a twitch to my shoulders.

'Yes, Father – that,' I said. 'Oh yes, I know what you're all thinking – Nancy's having another one of her panics. Nancy's blowing her top again and making a drama out of nothing.

'Well, never mind that, you're saying to yourselves – all we do is sit and smile at her and humour her . . .'

'No, Nancy, no. It's not like that,' said Rosie softly. 'You have your say. Talk to us. We'll listen.

'We need to know. And we need you, Nancy. We always have done.'

I was completely taken aback. I was stopped dead in full flow. I was like one of William's silly locomotives from the Great Eastern Railway crashing into the swing bridge at Beccles and feeling an utter chump.

I sort of flustered and fluttered and said:

'Yes. Well.'

But then I breathed in deeply and composed myself like I'd been taught to do before going on stage at the golf club Christmas panto and said:

'All I want to say is this – we've always been a united family, haven't we?'

'That's right,' said Rosie, calm as you like once again.

I ignored it. Completely. I continued.

'We've had our ups and downs,' I said. 'My God, have we had our ups and downs – quarrels, tantrums, hysterics, panics, the whole works. But we've always been united. Right?'

'Right,' said Rosie.

'So all I want to know is what's going on?' I said. 'Why are we cracking up?'

No one spoke.

I turned to Rosie and said:

'Well?'

She did not answer.

I turned to Father and William and said:

'What about you two?'

They said nothing.

'I see,' I said. 'I see. It's Winston, isn't it? Winston's behind all this. It's Winston who's trying to destroy us.

'Yes, Rosie? Yes, William?'

No one spoke. But they did not try to hide away from my gaze. They just stared at me impassively.

'I'll try to be cool, calm and collected,' I said. 'Since Winston came to live in this house our lives have changed out of all recognition. Of course, at first you all wanted to throw him out. You were all clamouring for it.'

'I wasn't,' said Rosie.

'Oh yes you were,' said William.

'No, I was not,' said Rosie.

'Shut up,' I shouted. 'Shut up, shut up, shut up.'

Rosie looked daggers at William, and he pouted his lower lip and stared at her out of the tops of his eyes.

Back to normal. Good. I was in control again.

'Thank you very much,' I said. 'I'll continue. As I was saying – you all wanted to get rid of Winston. And now what? Rosie's in the garden, whispering to him, cuddling him, holding his hand, wanting to leave us and set up home in London. And William's mooning around all day long.'

'I am not mooning,' said William. 'I'm thinking.'

'Thinking about what?' I said with a snap of triumph. 'Thinking about deserting us?'

That struck home. Oh yes, it plunged right into his miserable, pathetic little vitals.

'Yes – well – yes,' he mumbled.

I returned to the attack.

'Good Lord, even Father's changed,' I said. 'He's stopped telling us his interminably long and boring stories about India.'

'That's only because I've got another string to my bow, Nancy,' said Father calmly.

'What other string to your bow?' I said.

'Interminably long and boring stories about the Davis Cup.'

'The Davis Cup?' said William with a scarcely controlled tremble to his voice.

'Yes,' said Father. 'It's a fact not generally known that in the year 1966 India reached the final challenge round of the Davis Cup when they were defeated by Australia in Melbourne.

'Or was it Adelaide?

'The point is that . . .'

I couldn't help myself. It just came blurting out and I bellowed.

'Shut up, Father. Shut up, shut up.'

It had the desired effect.

They shut up.

I looked at them, and this time they averted their gaze from me.

Good. I was ready to get down to the nitty-gritty of the proceedings. Thank goodness I had had the foresight to wear those pearls Mother won at golf in Birkdale all those years ago.

I straightened my shoulders, set my nose at a haughty angle and said:

'I do not intend to play the role of martyr, but it is a simple fact that I have sacrificed the best part of my life devoting myself entirely to your interests.

'I am not asking you to say yes or to say no. There is no need, because deep down in your hearts you know that it's true.

'Well, my dear family, that sacrifice is not going to be wasted. Do you understand that? I am not going to waste all those years of dedicating myself solely to your welfare. I am not going to let them go without a fight.

'So listen to me very carefully.

'Like it or not, my dears, our lives are inextricably bound together. As individuals we could not exist on our own. We would die.

'Ah yes, you've all got your dreams. I know you've got them.

'Look at Rosie – glamorous job in London. Her own flat. Handsome young men begging for her favours. Independence. Freedom. Mistress of her destiny.

'Sounds wonderful, doesn't it, Rosie? Sounds sublime.

'But you wouldn't survive it for a week.

'At the first hint of happiness, the first sign of contentment you'd come bolting back to the family, clamouring for its disputes, craving for the quarrels and the conflicts. Grovelling on your hands and knees for them. Pleading for them.

'Rosie, my sweet younger sister, you cannot survive without us.

'Yes? Am I right?'

She did not speak. Not a word.

'And what about you, William?' I said. 'What are you hatching up, my lovely brother? What little plans has Winston sowed into that starched and stiff and prim imagination of yours?'

'Winston has nothing to do with what I feel,' said William hotly. 'And I have to say here and now that I take the strongest possible exception to the tone and manner of your attitude.'

'Don't be so bloody pompous,' snapped Rosie. 'Shut up and let her speak.'

She turned to me and said softly:

'Go on, Nancy.'

I paused for a moment, and then I said:

'I love you, William. I really love you. And you need my love. Oh, boy, do you need my love.

'You need my love. You need Rosie's contempt. You need Father's indifference.

'Without your daily dose of that, my sweet, you'd die.'

He seemed to crumple before my eyes. He looked just like a discarded raincoat in a prep school cloakroom.

I turned to Father and said:

'And you, Father? What about you?'

'Oh, I'm soldiering on, Nancy. Soldiering on. I used to say that to your mother when she was alive and we lived in Calcutta.

'Or was it Cawnpore?'

There was a sudden flash of anger from William.

'Who cares?' he said. 'Who the hell cares? I'm sick and tired of listening to his bloody stories.'

I raised my hand like I used to do at the school debating society and he fell silent.

'Carry on, Father,' I said gently. 'Tell us about Calcutta or was it Cawnpore. We're all ears.'

Father lit up his pipe, adjusted his spats and said:

'Well, I remember this day particularly well. It's etched deep in my memory. It was a Sunday.

'Or was it Wednesday?

'I don't suppose it matters much really.

'The point is we had a fire in the kitchen.

'Fearfully inconvenient. The whole place burned down. The cook wallah for some unaccountable reason took umbrage and attacked the ablutions wallah with a whopping great cleaver.

'Frightful din they kicked up till the police came and belaboured them with their staves.

'We had to have a cold lunch that day, and we'd hardly got stuck in to the asparagus when the roof caved in during an electrical storm, the

88

police 'phoned to say they'd charged the cook with murder and your mother was rushed to hospital with acute appendicitis.

'And when I visited her for the first time two or three days later, she smiled at me warmly and with most commendable thoughtfulness asked me how I was coping.

'And I took my pipe out of my mouth, tapped it on her bedhead and said: "Oh, don't bother about me, old horse, I'm soldiering on." '

There was silence.

The carriage clock on the mantelpiece clicked his tired old tick. A gust of wind billowed out the curtains. In the distance a deer barked.

And then very quietly and very softly Rosie said:

'All right. You win. I stay.'

'What?' said William.

Rosie turned to him with fire roaring in her eyes.

'I said, I'm staying,' she said. 'Now that's enough. There's no more to be said. The subject is closed.

'I'm staying here.

'The family is united.

'God rot your souls.'

There were tears streaming down her cheeks as she stormed out of the room and slammed the door violently behind her.

After a moment Father tapped out his pipe in the bowl of ready-salted potato crisps and said:

'And when I got back from hospital, they told me war had been declared.'

17

I couldn't sleep that night.

The rain drummed at the window panes and the wind rattled at the shutters with the hint of winter on its breath.

I tossed and I turned.

I thought of Rosie when she was born. She looked furious. She looked livid. When I saw her for the first time in Mother's arms all crinkled and wrinkled, she had this look on her face as much as to say:

'Why me? Why should this have happened to me? I didn't ask to be born.'

She hadn't changed.

And then I thought of William when he was a little boy with baggy khaki shorts flapping below his knees and his black plimsolls and his Aertex shirt and his Fair Isle pullover and his big ears.

He always looked so puzzled.

He always had a frown on his face. I remember once taking him to see the trains on Darlington station, and I said to him:

'What do you want to be when you grow up, William?'

And he said:

'I want to be a pirate and I want to have adventures and I want to marry a princess and write story books about engine drivers and be a famous writer and live in a big house with Lawrence of Arabia and O. S. Nock.'

And then he clutched my hand tightly and smiled his puzzled smile and said:

'But I don't suppose I ever will.'

He hadn't changed.

Next morning Winston came up to me as I was in the garden pruning the roses.

He stared at me silently for a moment with his great gnarled scarred brown hands resting on his hips.

Then he said:

'I'm taking you out for dinner, Nancy. For lunch sort of thing.'

I curled my lips at him and said:

'I'm afraid it's inconvenient just at the moment, Winston. Some other time, maybe.'

Winston did not change the expression on his face. He did not remove his hands from his hips.

He just said in a firm, controlled voice:

'I'll have my motor, my car, at the front door in half an hour's time. Go and get washed, comb your hair, squirt yourself with scent and be there.

'Half an hour.

'Right?'

And I did as I was told.

And Winston was waiting for me at the front door.

He was wearing a double-breasted blue blazer, a cream shirt with a pink neckerchief and sleek silver-grey flannel trousers.

He'd cut himself on the neck with his razor, and there was a sliver of blood-soaked toilet paper stuck to the wound. I wanted to caress it with my lips.

I got into his motor, his car, and we drove off.

It was the most perfect day. We didn't speak. Gulls yapped. Shire horses whinnied.

The rain had disappeared. The wind had whisked winter away and autumn stretched its long lazy arms over the countryside.

We drove over the smooth, silky shoulders of the downs. We dropped down into the dark, smouldering flanks of the valley.

We stopped at a pub on the banks of a chalk stream.

I sat in the garden. It had ornamental herons made of stone and an aviary with tropical birds. They glittered like jewels and sang like angels and pecked each other viciously when no one was looking.

Winston went to the bar and returned with a pint of bitter, a glass of grapefruit crush and a plate of venison sandwiches with great dollops of home-made peach chutney and rowan jelly.

He stared at me silently for a moment.

He drank his pint in a single gulp. He went for another. He took a small, neat fastidious sip from it with his little finger crooked.

And then he said:

'So Rosie ain't leaving?'

'Apparently not,' I said, all neat and fastidious.

'Why ain't she leaving, Nancy?'

'I really haven't the faintest idea, Winston,' I said. 'And I certainly don't think it's any concern of yours.'

'No?' said Winston.

'No.'

Winston offered me the plate of sandwiches. I declined. He picked up three, stuffed them into his mouth and gobbled them up like a half-crazed cement mixer.

If he'd done that at my private grammar school, he'd have had his wrists slapped and his hockey stick confiscated for a week.

He wiped a slurp of peach chutney from his chin. He narrowed his eyes and he said:

'You thinks you got me beat, don't you, Nancy? You thinks you got old Winston whacked.'

'Nothing of the sort, Winston,' I said. 'You don't come into it.'

'No?'

'No.'

Firmness, confidence – that was the way to treat him.

How could he compete against me in the sophistication stakes? I'd been to the National Theatre and seen Albert Finney. I hadn't understood a word he'd said, but at least I'd seen him. And I'd seen the sun set on the naked shoulders of the Matterhorn. And I'd heard the jingle of the harnesses of the white horses at the Spanish Riding School. And I'd smelled the armpits of fishermen hauling their boats ashore on the Costa Brava before it became common.

I was in command. I was mistress of the situation just like Queen Elizabeth before the Spanish Armada, which was in 1588. I was the cool, calm eye at the centre of the gathering storm.

And then Winston said quite casually:

'But I loves you, Nancy.'

Instantly the blood rushed to my head. The wolves and hyenas howled at my eardrums. I felt a clawing tightening of my berdongers, my breasts, and I said weakly:

'No, you don't.'

'Oh yes, I does, Nancy,' said Winston with an intensity that blazed in his eyes and shimmered in his voice. 'Without a doubt I loves you and desires you.'

I struggled with the weak little voice which cried out deep in my heart. I plunged deep into the depths of experience I had gained from all those years with the St John's Ambulance and the meals on wheels and I said in a severe, cold-rimmed voice:

'Now, you listen to me, Winston. It's high time we stopped all this nonsense.'

'Nonsense, Nancy?'

'Nonsense, Winston,' I said firmly. 'You made matters perfectly clear to me the day you moved into the house, which was very much against my will, as you know only too well.'

'Do I, Nancy?'

'Yes, you do. You told me that you were hellbent on getting rid of my sister and my brother and my father so you and I could live alone and together in the house.'

'Course I did, Nancy. Without a doubt I did.'

'Well, it won't work, Winston. It will not work. Rosie will not move. William won't move. And Father is quite incapable of moving.

'The family is going to stay together and there is not a thing you can do about it.'

'No, Nancy?' said Winston.

'No, Winston,' I said. 'No, no, no.'

There was a sudden commotion in the aviary. Feathers flew. There were the most ghastly squawks and screeches. How could such beautiful, exquisite creatures make such hideous, blood-chilling noises? A drab little bird with a plumage of dull grey and dirty brown sat placidly on a perch preening itself as the mayhem swooped and squabbled around it. Then in an instant it was over. The drab grey bird looked calmly at his mate and pecked her viciously on the back.

And at the same time Winston leaned forward and said:

'Do you remember the day of the village fete last year, Nancy?'

Another cold dagger thrust deep into my ribs. Another distant howl of the slavering wolves.

'What?' I said.

'The village fete, Nancy?' he said. 'I'm asking if you remembers it.'

'Well – well, yes. Bits and bobs, I suppose.'

'Not bits and bobs, Nancy. You remembers every single item of it,' he said, reaching across the table and taking hold of my hand. 'In the morning you was crying. I didn't see you. I didn't come anywhere near you that morning, but I knew you was crying.

'And in the afternoon I found you pressed into the old holly bush at the side of the meadow where they was holding the fete and you was shivering and I took hold of your hand and I led you to my motor, my car, and I drove you to the wood at the back of my house.'

'Winston. Please.'

'And I helped you out of the car and I took you through the wood to the little glade with the willow bane and the coltsfoot. And you was wearing a wide black skirt and a white blouse. And we sat down side by side beneath the old beech tree and I said to you: "You ain't never had a man before, has you, Nancy?" '

'Please, Winston. Please, don't go on.'

He held my hand more tightly and he said:

'And I pressed myself into you, Nancy. And I kissed you on the cheek. And while I was kissing you I opened the buttons on the front of your blouse and . . .'

I snatched my hand away from him and I shouted:

'That's enough, Winston. Stop it. Stop it at once.'

And then my shoulders crumpled and I whispered:

'Please, Winston. Please, please.'

Winston took hold of my hand again. He stared straight into my eyes and he said:

'And when I come round to see you next morning with a drainpipe for your outside bogs, you looked at me and your whole face was beaming and you shouted at the top of your voice: "I'm happy. I'm happy, I'm happy." '

I couldn't move my eyes from his gaze. The Zapata moustache. The sliver of blood-soaked toilet paper on his neck. The deep brown eyes glowing with love.

Very softly I said:

'And I was happy, Winston. I was.'

'And you can be happy again, Nancy.'

'But I am happy, Winston. Can't you understand that? I'm happy keeping the family together. That's where my happiness lies.'

'Happiness, Nancy?'

'Happiness, Winston.'

'Ah, but there's happiness and happiness, ain't there, Nancy? To one man happiness is writing a Beethoven concerto. To another it's having a good satisfying bowel movement. And who is to say, Nancy, that Beethoven didn't get more pleasure out of having a good stiff crap than in writing the *Moonlight Sonata*?'

Despite myself I couldn't help laughing.

'Oh, Winston,' I said. 'Winston Hayballs, you are absolutely incorrigible.'

'That I am, Nancy. That I am without a doubt.'

He took hold of my other hand. He pressed it to his heart and he said so earnestly, so sincerely that my heart sang and soared:

'I loves you, Nancy. I desires you. I wants you. And you can be sure of this – when old Winston wants something, he surely gets it finally and in the end look.

'Oh yes, indeed he does. Without a doubt.'

We drove home in silence.

Winston cooked me sweetbreads in mustard gravy and summer pudding for my supper, which I took alone in my sewing room. I listened to Beethoven's *Moonlight Sonata* on the gramophone and then I went to bed.

I slept soundly.

I dreamed of chalk streams and ornamental herons. I dreamed of yapping gulls and shire horses whinnying. I dreamed of a holly bush and a glade with willow bane and coltsfoot. I dreamed of the great shifting, whispering, shimmering canopy of a beech tree looking deep down into my eyes.

And when I awoke, the first words I said were:

'I'm sure Beethoven wasn't at all like that.'

And I was happy.

I was happy as I dusted the bedrooms. I was happy as I worked on the new cushions in my sewing room. I was happy as I arranged the flowers in the drawing room, the sitting room.

And then I saw them.

Winston and Rosie.

They were walking down the front drive. They were walking hand in hand.

Rosie was wearing her royal-blue velvet pantaloons and her pearl-grey cashmere sweater, and her blonde hair was loose and free.

And Winston was wearing a double-breasted navy-blue blazer, a cream shirt with a pink neckerchief and sleek silver-grey flannel trousers.

And they drove off in his motor.

In his car.

What on earth was he up to now?

18

What Winston was up to was simple:

He took Rosie to a public house.

'What a lovely pub, Winston,' said Rosie.

'Not bad, eh, Rosie? You don't mind sitting in the garden?'

'Of course not, Winston. It's wonderful. Are those flamingos over there?'

'No, Rosie. They're ornamental herons look. And them birds scratching at the bottom of the aviary are tropical birds sort of thing – ornamental quail to be precise. Only they're made of flesh and blood, and them herons are made of concrete freshly knocked off from Tommy Leonard's builder's yard.'

Rosie chuckled.

'Fancy you knowing a thing like that, Winston,' she said.

'Oh, I knows everything what goes on round here, Rosie. That I do without a doubt.'

Rosie took a bite from her venison sandwich and a sip from her gin and tonic and said:

'Well then, Winston, cheers. And thanks for bringing me to this smashing pub.'

'You're very welcome, Rosie,' said Winston. And then he smiled and said: 'Do you know, this is the first time I've ever took one of my bits of fluff to this pub.'

'Then I'm flattered, Winston.'

Winston took a long sup of his pint of bitter. He smacked his lips thoughtfully, straightened the knot in his pink neckerchief and said:

'So, Rosie, you ain't going to London then?'

'That's right, Winston – I ain't going to London.'

'Why?'

Rosie flicked her shoulders and said quickly:

'I don't want to talk about it.'

Winston paused for a moment. He nodded his head slowly and then he said:

'Rosie.'

'Yes?'

'Rosie Empson, you just look at me straight in the eyes and you tell me firm and plain and truthful why you ain't going to London.'

He stretched out across the table and took hold of her hand.

'Tell me, Rosie,' he said. 'Tell old Winston the truth.'

Rosie hung her head and after a while she said softly:

'Because of Nancy.'

'Say it again.'

Rosie looked at him straight in the eyes, and her nostrils flared and the tawny tints in her long golden hair flashed as she shook her head.

'Because of Nancy,' she snapped. 'God damn you – it's always because of Nancy. Everything we do in this family is for the sake of Nancy.

'Oh, outsiders don't know it. They haven't a clue.

'They look at us and they think to themselves – poor, noble, long-suffering Nancy. She's sacrificed the best years of her life pampering and cosseting that dreadful family of hers. Sweet, gentle Nancy. She's a saint. She's a real saint.

'Bollocks.

'She's not, Winston. Far from it.'

'No?' said Winston.

Rosie lifted up her head and knocked back her glass of gin and tonic. She slammed it down hard on the table.

And then it all came flooding out.

'No, Winston, Nancy is not a saint,' she said. 'Nancy is a selfish, thoughtless, domineering bitch. And she always has her way. Always, always.

'Everything that anyone does in this family is for Nancy. We must keep Nancy happy. We mustn't upset Nancy.

'All those moves we made? They weren't because of Father. Oh no, they were because of Nancy. And when we were settling in, enjoying ourselves, finding new friends, she'd up and off and make the excuse of Father's health.

'And why? I'll tell you.

'Because if we were happy, we'd fall apart. And Nancy's one role in life is keeping us together. Stop that, and her life is ruined. She's destroyed.

'And so, Winston, that is why Nancy always gets her way.

'And that is why I am not going to London – because of bloody Nancy.'

Winston waited for her distress to subside and then he said, squeezing her hand tightly:

'But you can serve Nancy better by going to London, Rosie. You can do her the greatest favour what you've ever done her in the whole of your life.'

'What?'

'I'll tell you something, Rosie, what I never told no one before,' said Winston. 'You remember the day of the village fete last year?'

'Yes.'

'And do you remember that Nancy went missing all afternoon?'

'Yes.'

'And I was missing, too, wasn't I, Rosie?'

'Yes. Yes, you were.'

'Well, Nancy and me was together.'

'What?'

'I took her to the wood at the back of my house, Rosie, and we lay together under the old beech tree and we ... well, you know what I mean, Rosie? We done it.'

'What?' said Rosie. 'You done it? With Nancy?'

'Oh yes, Rosie, without a shadow of a doubt.'

Winston took his hand away from Rosie, leaned back in his chair and sighed deeply.

'The trouble is, Rosie, I don't reciprocate look. I don't love her one little scrap. It's you what I loves, Rosie.'

'What?'

'It is you what I loves, Rosie,' said Winston. 'And one day very soon old Winston's going to have to tell the whole wide world. And if he does that, can you imagine what it will do to Nancy?

'She loves me, see, Rosie. She worships the ground what I treads on sort of thing.

'She wants me, Rosie. She desires me. She loves me.

'And if you wasn't round here to tempt me with your temptations, well, I reckons one day in the fullness of time I could find feelings for her and . . . and . . . we might . . . well, we might . . .'

'Do it again?'

'Not on my part, Rosie. Not on my part. But I might not be able to help myself, would I?'

Rosie did not speak.

She ran her forefinger round the rim of her glass. She looked at the dull grey bird in the aviary nibbling contentedly at its mate's neck.

Then she said:

'I don't know what to say, Winston.'

Winston smiled broadly.

'There's nothing to say, Rosie. But there's plenty to do,' he said. 'Oh yes, Rosie, without a doubt, there's plenty for you to do.'

19

Without comment.

Without one single word of comment.

That evening I was in the sitting room, reading my women's magazine.

William sat on the piano stool, making notes in his silly little school exercise book.

Father sat in the winged armchair by the fire polishing the silver band on his pipe with spit and the sleeve of his shirt.

Then Rosie entered the room through the french windows.

'I've an announcement to make,' she said.

'Well, go on, Rosie, tell us,' I said. 'There's no need to be all stiff and formal about it.'

'I've decided to take that job in London,' she said.

'What?' I said.

'I don't intend to discuss it, Nancy. I don't intend to state my reasons. But I am going to London, and that is that.'

'Can I come with you, Rosie?' said William.

'What?' said Rosie.

'Let me come with you, Rosie,' said William eagerly. 'We can share a flat together, and I'll do the cooking and the cleaning and the ironing, when I'm not having adventures with pirates and wild, rampant women and . . .'

And I screamed at the top of my voice:

'Oh, my God. Oh, my God.'

A helicopter roared overhead.

When it passed by, there was silence, and Father said:

'Helicopters again. Whacko. Jolly Dee. Been a fearfully pleasant day. Or has it been a bloody awful day? What do you think, Nancy, old boy?'

As I said – no comment.

Not a single word of comment.

20

The sun was still shining.

Idle, boastful swine – couldn't it find anything more useful to do with itself?

I was in the corridor outside the drawing room, the sitting room, hoovering.

I've always liked hoovering.

It's so restful, so peaceful, so tranquil, so wonderfully contemplative.

I've always thought there should be a Roman Catholic order – The Little Sisters of the Hoover.

They'd live in a simple, white-washed convent in a broad, winding, herb-scented valley overlooked by towering snow-capped mountain peaks. And there'd be tawny goats in the fields and dippers and grey wagtails in the clattering river.

And the convent would be full of Chinese rugs and Wilton carpets and Laura Ashley curtains and foam-backed underfelt, and the little sisters would spend all their days from sunup to sundown hoovering them and praying for us poor souls who struggle wearily through our lives pampering and cosseting a foul-tempered sister, a weak-gutted brother and a father who slucks into the depths of his disgusting pipe all day long and tears holes in his sheets with the buckles of his spats.

I switched off the hoover and I heard them, my precious family. They were squabbling. As usual. As always. And then their voices were drowned by the clattering of a helicopter.

What on earth were they talking about this time?

What were they plotting against me?

Nancy Empson, spinster and fortyish, put her ear to the door, but she could not hear them as they talked.

'I say, another helicopter. Whacko. Jolly Dee,' said Father. 'That's the fifth this morning.'

Rosie stamped her feet and shook her fist and shouted at the helicopter:

'Shut up. Shut up, you noisy sod.'

The noise died away and Rosie said:

'Bloody helicopter! I swear the only reason I'm clearing out of here and going back to London is those disgusting helicopters!'

'I know, Rosie, I won't miss them either,' said William. 'Now the thing is, when we buy our house, we must make sure that we're not on the flight path to Heathrow.'

'William, you and I are not buying a house together,' said Rosie, flaring her nostrils and glowering. 'If you want to break free from here and go to London, fine. That's your business. But you are not living with me.'

'Why not?'

'Because the whole point of my moving is so I can be independent for the first time in my life. I can break free of the shackles of this God-awful family.'

'But that's precisely why I want to move, Rosie,' said William. 'So we can share a house and we can both be independent together.'

Rosie crumpled up her silk handkerchief in her tight-clenched fists and said:

'William, you are absolutely impossible.'

'No, I'm not,' said William. 'I'm being very sensible. I'm being practical.'

'You're being a prize prat.'

'Oh no, I'm not.'

'Oh yes, you are.'

'I'm not.'

'You are.'

The helicopter rumbled and roared overhead again and Father smiled deeply and said:

'Here we go again, chaps. Another helicopter. Fearfully pleasant, don't you think?'

At this William and Rosie turned and both bellowed at the tops of their voices:

'Shut up, Father. Shut up.'

We were what is called a happy family. And now we were splitting up. Rosie was going to live in London. And so was William.

Which left just me and Father.

What a deliciously gorgeous prospect. How exciting and fulfilling were the years stretching ahead of me.

Washing the skid marks out of an old man's underpants. Listening to his interminable, gripingly boring stories of his days in India. Taking the pipe out of his mouth when he fell asleep and showered the front of his cardigan with burning sparks. Cutting his toenails. Shaving him. Bathing him. Wiping his bottom. Cleaning his spectacles so he could read the obituaries in *The Daily Telegraph*.

I'd failed them.

I'd failed myself.

All those years my only talent in life had been keeping the family together.

And it was all cracking up, and I'd failed.

I thought of the white-washed convent and the dippers and the grey wagtails and I said a little prayer.

After I'd finished the hoovering, I mucked out Father's bedroom and polished William's stapling machine in his study. I went to my sewing room for half an hour's unprovoked criticism of my new Jilly Cooper.

I'd only been at it five minutes when I looked up and saw Rosie approaching Winston in the garden.

Oh my God, more intrigue.

'Hello there, Rosie,' said Winston. 'What do you reckon?'

'Not a lot,' said Rosie.

Winston picked a drowsy wasp off the side of his wellington, pinched its head and flicked it with his thumbnail into the clump of straggle-headed achillea.

Then he smiled and said:

'Well, Rosie, my old wingsy bash, he's a fine day today without a doubt. He's a real bramah of a day, ain't he?'

'Mm,' said Rosie.

She hesitated for a moment, and then she said:

'Winston?'

'Yes, Rosie?' said Winston brightly.

'Are you sure I'm doing the right thing moving to London?'

'Course I am, Rosie. Not getting cold feet, are you?'

'No.'

'Then why do you ask? Why do you inquire sort of thing?'

'It's Nancy.'

'What about Nancy?'

'It's her face, Winston. It's the look in her eyes – pain, sadness, accusation.

'I'm leaving. I'm destroying her family. I'm destroying her. I can't bear it. It's ripping me apart. I lie awake all night and every morsel and fraction of the house screams at me that I'm ruining her life.'

'No, you ain't Rosie,' said Winston softly. 'That you ain't to be sure. Remember what I told you in the pub with them ornamental herons and the tropical birds?'

'Yes.'

Winston put his arm round her shoulders and hugged her.

'Well, always keep that right in the forefront of your mind, Rosie, my lovely, lustrous young darling,' he said. 'Keep repeating it: "Winston loves Rosie. But Nancy loves Winston. Winston don't want Rosie to go, but if she stays, she'll destroy Nancy's love for Winston." '

Rosie looked down at her feet and nodded her head weakly.

'And what would Nancy do then if her love was destroyed, Rosie?' said Winston. 'What would her life be then without old Winston to pamper her and cosset her and cuddle her tight and warm beneath the old beech tree in the wood at the back of his house?'

Rosie looked up at Winston. She stretched out her hand and gently stroked his cheek.

'I know what you say, Winston,' she said. 'I understand.'

Winston smiled, took hold of her hand and kissed it.

'Then just keep saying to yourself, Rosie – Winston loves Rosie. But

Nancy loves Winston. So Rosie's got to go to London, if he don't want to destroy Nancy.

'Simple, ain't it, Rosie? Very simple without a shadow of a doubt.'

I watched them together in the garden, Winston and Rosie.

I looked at them intently, saw their closeness and their warmth and their ease with each other. And I thought there might have been just a teeny-weeny bit between them.

No. It was absolutely preposterous.

What could a beautiful, talented, warm and witty young woman like Rosie possibly have seen in a fat, beer-swilling, belching, farting, blunt-thumbed, coarse, vulgar, stinking yob of a village poacher?

No, he'd never have dared set his sights so high. It would never have occurred to him.

And me?

What about me?

He told me he loved me.

And that was absolutely preposterous, too.

I was a mature woman. An educated woman. I'd been to private school on the South Coast and won prizes for domestic science and natural history.

I was a widely travelled woman. I'd been to the Prado in Florence, even though the pictures were far too cocky with themselves for my liking. I'd seen the Lorelei on the Rhine and heard all those disgusting Germans with their square heads and their fat necks and their ghastly wives with pink eyelids and waddling bottoms, crying into their beer as the ship passed beneath the rock. I'd been to the Nyphenburg Gardens in Vienna and fed the red squirrels with squashed-up pretzels.

And I was still a beautiful woman.

I didn't sag – well, nowhere you'd notice, nowhere you could see and, after all, no one's perfect.

My back was straight. My bosom was firm. My legs were long and slim and shapely. I'd still got all my own teeth.

What did I want with a leering, drink-sodden lout with his long, greasy hair and his tattoos over his nipples and his dirty slimy teeth and his flapping wellingtons covered in over-ripe cow pats?

And then I paused.

I looked out of the window and saw Winston sitting side by side with Rosie on the stone bench in the rose arbour and stroking her long, golden hair and said out loud:

'Winston! Oh, Winston, what are you doing to us?'

We had poached halibut for dinner followed by a damson flan, wickedly tart and darkly sensuous in its juicy depths.

I went to sleep listening to Beethoven on the BBC Third Programme and the reception was very good considering.

Next morning I had boiled pheasants' eggs and wholemeal brown toast dripping with white butter and oozing with wild, downland honey.

I went into the kitchen and it was cool and mellow out of the rays of the boastful, braggart autumn sun.

I was alone. It was lovely. It was so peaceful, so tranquil, so contemplative.

I thought back to all those blessed, precious moments of peace and tranquillity when I was younger.

Standing hand in hand with the golf professional from the Dukeries in the dog leg of the short fourteenth and listening to the whispering of the dusk. Polishing the wing mirrors of the Morgan three-wheeler in the West Country and polishing the spokes of the wire wheels with a wad of Duraglit and looking up and seeing out of the corner of my eye the producer in his pink fisherman's smock gazing down at me from his mother's bedroom window. Throwing sticks for Wynford on the lonely, muddy, hummocky shore at Silverdale and seeing the peregrines stoop and wheel at the flocks of sanderling and dunlin, or whatever they call themselves.

Lying side by side with Winston under the old beech tree in the wood at the back of his house and hearing his regular, heavy, sated breathing and listening to the crooning echoes of lust and passion in my loins.

How lovely it was to be alone in the shadowed kitchen with its copper pots and pans nodding solemnly to themselves on the hooks above the old range and the old colander gloating with its booty of fresh-chopped parsley and basil.

And then William walked in.

He did not look at me. He did not speak. He opened the door of the utility room, where I could hear Winston singing to himself, and clamped it firmly shut behind him.

Oh God, more of it.

'Ah, there you are, Winston,' said William. 'Not disturbing you, am I?'

'No,' said Winston. 'I'm just ironing a pair of Nancy's knickers.'

'Good, good,' said William, rocking up and down on the balls of his heels. 'Do you like ironing, Winston?'

'Not bad. What I likes most about it is the constant spitting on the bottom of the iron sort of thing.'

'Do you think I'd be able to do it, Winston? I mean, when I go to London, I'll have to fend for myself as regards the domestic chores, won't I?'

'Oh yes, William, that you will without a doubt, my old wingsy bash.'

William sighed and scratched his pate.

'That's what bothers me, you see, Winston,' he said. 'If I've got all the domestic chores to do, how on earth will I find time to finish my book on the Light Railways of County Antrim?'

'But you ain't going to London to write books about railways, William. You're going to London to have wild and wicked adventures and write books about birds with big bristols look.'

'Yes, I know,' said William, tugging at the damp cuffs of his oatmeal cardigan. 'But if I'm ironing and washing all day, how will I ever meet these birds with big ... with big you-know-whats?'

'Simple, William. You lives with Rosie.'

'But she won't have me.'

'What?'

'She refuses point blank to let me live with her.'

'Hold on a mo, William. Do you mind getting out of my light while I deal with this frilly bit on the end of the right leg?'

'Certainly,' said William, moving out of the light. 'Is that better?'

'Perfectly, my old pile of rabbit tod,' said Winston, spitting on the bottom of the iron and holding it up to his cheek for an instant. 'Now then – you was saying?'

'I was saying that Rosie won't let me live with her,' said William. 'She's adamant. She says she wants her independence. She says I'd be under her feet all day, twittering and fussing. She said she'd have to look after me just the same as Nancy does.

'But she won't, Winston. She won't.

'I am perfectly capable of standing on my own two feet. Why does everyone think I'm useless? I got at least three badges when I was in Boy Scouts. I would have got a fourth only I lost my way in the map-reading test.

'I bitterly resent all this ridicule heaped upon me. I'm fed up of being bossed around by Nancy, being told when to change my shirts, when to start wearing woolly vests in the autumn, when it's safe to go out without a raincoat, having to take those beastly Gregory Powders laxative tablets every Friday night.

'I am perfectly capable, Winston, of standing on my own two feet.

'And that is why it is essential that I live with Rosie in London.'

Winston folded up neatly the last of Nancy's knickers.

He placed them carefully on the pile of underslips and nighties and stood back to admire his handiwork, sucking in deeply through the blue-chipped gap in his two front teeth.

Then he clapped William warmly on the shoulder and said:

'I'll have a word with her, William. You leave it to old Winston. He'll work things out for you. He always does.

'And whilst you're here, what about changing them underpants of yours. Dirty sod, you've had them on at least three weeks . . .'

'Oh, my God,' said William. 'Don't tell Nancy.'

21

I couldn't bear it.

I couldn't bear hearing Rosie singing to herself as she packed up her belongings in her studio.

I couldn't bear the smug look on William's face and the spring in his step.

I couldn't bear Father's shifty smirk and the clink of gin bottles in his jacket pocket as he plodded off each morning to his shed at the bottom of the garden.

And it was all the fault of Winston.

Winston manipulating them. Winston talking behind my back and setting them up against me. Winston giving them their independence from me.

Why didn't I throw him out?

I couldn't.

Why didn't I tell him he was the most disgusting, loathsome, contemptible man I had ever met in the whole of my life?

I couldn't.

Why didn't I tell him that the very sight of his body was repulsive to me?

I couldn't.

Why didn't I tell him that the day we lay side by side under the beech tree was the most horrific, nauseating, revolting, disgusting experience I had ever had apart from having two milk teeth taken out with gas by that German dentist at school with his smelly fountain pens and the green and yellow smears on his tongue?

I couldn't.

Why didn't I tell him I didn't love him, I didn't want him, I hated him, I despised him?

I couldn't.

I was on the patio watering the herb cuttings he'd planted earlier in the month. They looked so happy, so contented, so full of life.

Those gnarled brown scarred hands of his had set the juices running in their stems, brought vigour and vitality to their crackling leaves and their withered roots.

Oh, Winston, Winston, you took them from their dried-out, brown-curled newspaper packages and you renewed their spirit and their will to live.

Oh, Winston, Winston.

And then I saw him heading purposefully towards Father's shed at the bottom of the garden.

Not another stab in the back?

'Come on in, Winston,' said Father as Winston entered the shed. 'It's only me. Make yourself at home. Take a pew.'

'Ta very much,' said Winston. 'Do you fancy a slug of my gin?'

'I say, how fearfully pleasant of you. But only if we do it in secret. I'm a secret drinker, you know. Don't tell anyone, will you?'

'I thinks they already knows.'

'Well, so long as they keep it secret, that's all right, isn't it? That's the secret of being a successful secret drinker.'

He took a swift draught from the bottle of gin, coughed and spluttered, giggled and then turned to Winston and said:

'Now then, Winston, old chap, I've asked you here for a conflab because I want to have a serious word with you.'

'Fire away,' said Winston. 'I'm all ears.'

'Well, you remember my idea of jiggering off to India? Well, it was your idea really, old chap, but since I've adopted it myself I rather like to think it was I who initiated it.'

'Quite right, too,' said Winston, helping himself to a quick glug from the bottle of gin.

Father looked at him beadily, snatched the bottle back and thrust it into his armpit beneath his jacket.

He smiled contentedly and said:

'Well then, Winston, I have to tell you in the strictest confidence that I have been to the bank, withdrawn all my savings and deposited them in a padlocked briefcase under the floorboards at the back of this shed.'

'I knows that,' said Winston. 'I was with you when you done it, you barmy old bugger.'

'Really, old chap?'

'Course I was. I drove you to the bank in my motor, my car. I waited outside while you collected your loot. I drove you back and it was me what prised up the floorboards and gave you the padlock for the briefcase.'

'How splendid. Fearfully pleasant to have such good company.'

'You're very welcome,' said Winston. 'Have another swig of gin.'

'I say, old chap. Thanks most awfully,' said Father, and he took the bottle from out of his jacket, supped at it blissfully and handed it to Winston.

Then he smiled and chuckled and said:

'Now then, Winston, what I have to say is this – I have now decided to take further action.'

'Which is?'

'To put into operation plans for jiggering off to India.'

'Good. I'm pleased to hear that, my old wingsy bash.'

'Now then, Winston, what I want you to do is this, old chap – I want you to go to our local branch of Thomas Cook and Sons Limited and ask if they've any idea of how a chap gets to India these days.'

'You goes by plane. From Heathrow Airport.'

'Ah,' said Father. 'Now we've hit the first snag. How does a chap get to Heathrow Airport?'

'I drives him there in my motor, my car.'

'Splendid. Now we're getting somewhere,' said Father. 'Now for the next problem. When we get to Heathrow Airport, how do we know which will be the plane for India?'

'It'll be wrote up on its front on an indicator board.'

'I say, I didn't realize you were such a seasoned traveller.'

113

'Oh yes, without a doubt I am. I've travelled all over the place look. I once went to Barnstaple on the back of Betty Hayballs' tandem.'

'You sound just the sort of man I'm looking for. Why don't you come with me to India as my travelling companion, unpaid fly repellent and devoted luggage wallah, Winston?'

'No, ta very much,' said Winston. 'I reckons I wouldn't think much to India.'

'Why not, old chap? The little brown buggers there are most fearfully good at playing leg spin, you know.'

'That's as maybe, but what about the grub, the nosh?'

'What about it?'

'Look, I once had one of them take-away curries sort of thing in a packet from the supermarket. Cor blimey Charlie, talk about Mount Vesuvius and the eruption of Krakatoa – I couldn't sit on the back of Betty Hayballs' tandem in comfort for three weeks solid.'

'In that case, old chap, you're better off where you are,' said Father, emptying the bottle of gin with a grunt of satisfaction. 'Stay here. Don't be tempted, I beg you. Don't give into high-sounding blandishments or the honeyed words of silver tongues.'

'I won't.'

'Good. I'm pleased to hear it,' said Father, yawning and shaking his head. He smiled once more and said: 'Good. It's settled. I shall travel alone to India. And I shall inform my family of my decision tonight. Fearfully pleasant place, India. Did I ever tell you about that time your Mother and I were in Burma, when she was alive? We'd taken up with this tree surgeon chappie from Bridlington and . . . and . . .'

His eyes closed softly and he began to snore.

Very carefully Winston took the bottle of gin from his hands and held it up to the light.

There was not a drop remaining in it.

He smiled to himself and said gently:

'You poor old sod. You poor old bugger.'

22

That night I detected distinct signs of tension as we gathered in the dining room.

I'd a sixth sense for that sort of thing.

It was the same all those years ago just before Mother announced she'd decided to take a golfing holiday alone in Norway and Father locked himself away in his study and played his records of Flotsam and Jetsam all night at the tops of their voices.

It was the same in Fort William seconds before Mother answered the telephone in the draughty, sneaky-elbowed hall and whispered away glancing over her shoulders into the parlour and Father locked himself away in his study and played on the ukulele all night.

There was something in the air, and I knew for certain it was not going to be nice.

An army helicopter jangled and gackled and golloped overhead and Rosie smashed her fist on to the table and said:

'Oh God, another helicopter. They're coming out at night now. Why? There's no nude women in back gardens for them to ogle at.'

'They've probably got special night-seeing equipment,' said William.

'Don't be so ridiculous, William,' I said. 'Get on with your soup and stop slurping.'

'Sorry, Nancy,' said William.

I glanced over to Father, and instantly I knew it. There was the source of my tension, there was the focus for my sixth sense and its sly, wicked little voice.

Sure enough Father put down his spoon and said:

'I wonder if I could have your attention for a moment, chaps. I have an announcement to make.'

I moved in swiftly to intercept like I used to do when I played right back at hockey and Thelma Boardman used to trip over my stick on purpose.

'Yes, Father, yes,' I said. 'We know all about that. You've dropped your napkin on the floor again. Here. Use mine and make sure it's properly tucked in.'

'But that's not the announcement I was going to make, Nancy, old boy,' said Father plaintively. 'What I was going to say was . . .'

And Winston walked into the room pushing a laden trolley.

'Right then. Main course up,' he said. 'Eyes down for a full house.'

Rosie clapped her hands with delight and said:

'Winston, it looks superb. What is it?'

Winston bowed stiffly, extended his right arm to the trolley and said:

'Shoulder of veal *Hongroise* – which means it comes from Hungary though I can tell you authentic sort of thing that the veal was freshly nicked from the abattoir this morning by certain acquaintances of mine who shall be nameless on account of their anonymity.

'Now then, what you've got with it is cucumber Vichy, salad Clementine, caramelized new potatoes and a couple of hefty dollops of the ballotine of duck left over from last night cos you couldn't finish it look.

'So you can get cracking, can't you, and it's quite all right with me if you scoops up the gravy with your bread knives.'

We tucked in instantly. It was delicious. It was yummy yummy. Winston stood by the head of the trolley, chin held high, arms folded across his breast, heels tightly together, staring straight ahead of him.

Father scooped up the sauce from his plate with his bread knife, sucked it vigorously and then hammered on the table with the smoker's compendium Mother had bought in the professional's shop at Turnberry all those years ago.

'Right, everyone,' he said. 'I have an announcement to make.'

'We know, Father, we know,' said Rosie. 'You want the salt passed to you.'

'No, no, Rosie,' said Father. 'That's not the announcement I want to make. It's far more important than that.'

'Of course it is, Father,' said William. 'You want the pepper.'

'No, I do not,' said Father and there was a testiness in his voice I had not heard since he read the obituary of John Masefield in *The Daily Telegraph*. 'It's something very different.'

I smiled sweetly at him and said:

'Well then, Father, tell us what it is.'

He chuckled and said quite baldly without so much as a by your leave:

'I want to tell you that I am going to India.'

Rosie and William dropped their forks and cried:

'What?'

I was speechless.

I was totally unprepared for it. It was just like that time in Newmarket when Mother announced that she intended to take a bicycling holiday alone with the celebrated jockey Edgar Britt – stuck-up little short arse he was.

'What's that you said, Father?' I said between tightly clenched teeth. 'What did you just say?'

'I intend to travel to India, old boy,' said Father. 'And in the fullness of time I shall settle down in a bungalow in the Assam Hills with a slim young lady with almond eyes, silver bangles round her ankles and gynormous bristols.

'But you're not to worry, chaps. I know how to get there – they have the destination written in capital letters on the front of the aeroplane.'

'I don't believe this,' I said. 'Will someone please tell me that I'm hearing voices in my head.'

Winston did not shift his stance. He kept looking straight ahead as he said:

'No, you ain't, missus. What you heard is real and for true. Your father, your old dad, is going to India. That's right, ain't it, my old bacon balls?'

'It most certainly is, old boy,' said Father. 'Everything has been worked out in the most meticulous detail. I shan't be taking the piano with me, but I shall be taking my togs. Never underestimate the importance of togs on occasions such as these.

'Now then, I intend to take the Bakelite wireless with the defective knobs and travel to India in easy stages. I shall stop off in Chippenham

117

for three weeks, Salisbury for a month, Andover for a fortnight and London for a year in order to regroup.'

'And where will you stay in London, Father?' said William.

'With Rosie, old boy.'

'Oh no, you won't,' said Rosie fiercely. 'I'm not having you getting your feet established under my table. You'll be there for the duration.'

'Exactly,' said William. 'You'd spoil everything for us.'

'Us, William?' said Rosie.

'Yes,' said William. 'You and me. Well, you and I, if you want to go all grammatical and arty-farty.'

'Oh no, oh no, William. You are not living with me.'

'Why not?'

'Because you're not.'

'Why?'

'Because I say so.'

I could not contain myself. I shrieked at the top of my voice:

'For heaven's sake, will you please be quiet. Shut up.'

They fell silent. They looked at me sulkily and Father commenced to stuff his mouth with slices of cucumber and golden, glistening new potatoes.

'Thank you,' I said. And my voice was calm once more as I turned to Father and said: 'Father.'

'Yes, old boy?' said Father.

'Are you aware, totally aware, rationally aware, of what you have just said?'

'Course he isn't,' said Rosie. 'He's been at the gin again.'

'No I haven't,' said Father. 'Well, only in secret with Winston.'

My eyes narrowed. The muscles in my neck tautened. I held my elbows tightly to my side and I said:

'Ah, Winston, eh?'

'That's right, old boy,' said Father scooping up more sauce with his knife. 'Winston.'

I turned to Winston and I said very softly:

'Winston.'

'Yes, Nancy?' he said.

'You bastard,' I said very quietly. And then shrieked at the top of my voice: 'You bastard. You bloody great evil bastard.'

There was silence. No one moved.

And then Father said:

'And then I'll probably stay at Heathrow Airport for a couple of months to acclimatize.'

23

I had this vision of myself.

I was an old lady, very weak and very frail, but I'd still got all my own faculties.

And I was living in an old folks' home by the seaside.

It was very well appointed. The staff were courteous and attentive. We each had our own room with remote control colour television and fitted carpets. We were allowed our own personal mementos and souvenirs provided they didn't offend the doctor who visited twice a week in his vintage Riley Kestrel.

I was rather happy.

From the garden you could look out over the sea. There were cormorants sitting on the breakwater hanging out their wings to dry. And there were yachts with taut, stiff sails and a rusty dredger clanking itself to sleep.

If I turned my head to the right, I could see a little grove.

It was very well cared for.

There were miniature roses and bushes of rosemary and hissup and basil and variegated thyme.

And in the middle of the grove were three black urns.

On one was written:

'Rosie – died of anger.'

On another was written:

'William – died of bewilderment.'

And on the third was written:

'Father – missing, presumed still alive.'

And then I turned my head back again to look out over the bay. The cormorants had gone. So had the dredger and the yachts.

The sea was calm.

It was very calm indeed.

And then suddenly there was a ripple on the surface. Only a small ripple, but the herring gulls wheeled away and screamed with alarm.

And the ripple grew bigger.

The waters churned.

They hissed and spat and foamed.

A whirlpool was formed.

It spun and roared.

It spat out great vomits of fume.

And then from its dead centre there arose a figure.

A man.

He was naked.

The water streamed from his limbs.

It cascaded from him.

It glistened on his flesh.

And he raised his arms to the heavens.

And a great, towering grin came to his face.

And he bellowed at the top of his voice:

'Hello there, Nancy.

'What do you reckon?

'Not a lot.'

That's the vision I had of myself that night in the old Dower House in Winterleaf Gunner.

It was silent.

Everyone was asleep.

But I wasn't. I was wide awake.

I lay in my bed, secure and snug.

I didn't move a muscle.

I listened. I listened very hard.

The trees were sleeping. The voles were cowering in the meadows under the moon-shadows of the hunting owls. The river soothed the resting salmon.

Very quietly I pulled back the sheets from my bed. I tip-toed across the carpet to the door. I opened it. I stepped outside on to the landing.

A pause. I looked slowly from left to right. I listened again.

The boiler for the hot water was crooning softly to himself from his hutch outside the kitchen door. I loved that boiler. He was a friend, a real chum.

I could hear the faint rasp of the house spider's feet – the killer of the skirting boards. I loved the house spider. He was a friend, a real chum.

I began to walk along the landing.

Very slowly.

I stopped outside a bedroom door.

I opened it.

I stepped inside.

Softly I closed the door behind me.

I said very softly:

'Winston.'

He stirred in the pit of his bed.

He grunted sleepily.

'Mm? Mm? What's that?'

I whispered more urgently:

'Winston. Winston.'

Instantly he sprang awake, his eyes darting from side to side, his head hunched into his shoulders.

'Oh. Oh, it's you,' he said. 'Hello then, Nancy. What do you reckon?'

'Not a lot,' I said.

I pulled back the sheets and I slipped into bed beside him.

He was naked.

He was not wearing pyjamas.

I took hold of him.

Gently at first.

He grunted with pleasure. He groaned.

And then quite suddenly I gripped him hard, and I squeezed and I squeezed with all my might.

'Christ all bloody mighty, woman,' he howled. 'Mind my equipment, will you.'

I twisted at him. I yanked and I tugged.

'You bastard,' I shouted. 'You bastard.'

We struggled. We fought. He ripped away my hands. I scratched at his face. I clawed at his chest. I bit at his neck. I kicked and I pummelled.

And then I stopped.

We lay side by side, panting. The perspiration streamed and gurgled down our bodies.

And very quietly, very softly I said:

'You bastard. Oh, you bastard.'

There was a pause, and then he said:

'Mind if I has a fag, Nancy?'

'No,' I said. 'Do as you like.'

He reached out to the bedside table for his tin and rolled himself a cigarette. He struck a match and lit it. He drew in the smoke deeply and sighed.

'My first today,' he said. 'Or is it still yesterday?'

I felt the heat from his body. I felt his breath on my neck. I heard the beat of his heart. I smelled his earthiness and his wickedness and his gentleness and his loving.

'Why are you doing this to me, Winston?' I said.

'Doing what, Nancy?'

'You know.'

'I don't.'

'You do,' I said sharply

'Shush,' said Winston. 'You'll wake the cobwebs up.'

I waited for a moment and then I said:

'Why are you trying to destroy me, Winston?'

'I ain't trying to destroy you, Nancy. I'm doing all this for your own good.'

'My good?'

'Oh yes, missus. Without a doubt. I'm getting rid of all your family so's you and me can be together. So we can lay in bed like this night after night for ever and for ever and sometimes in the afternoon, too, if you so desires and wishes it.'

He turned to me and I said:

'Don't touch me there, Winston.'

He moved his hand away, took another puff at his cigarette and said:

'I knows what you thinks, Nancy. You thinks old Winston is doing this just for his own personal cravings and desires. But that ain't true, Nancy.

'Oh yes, I wants you right enough. And you wants me, too, look.

'But the others, they needs what I'm doing. They needs their independence, Nancy. Rosie, William, your old dad – they needs to get away and stand on their own two feet. They doesn't need all this cosseting and pampering what you gives them. It's bad for them. Unhealthy sort of thing.

'They needs to be themselves. They doesn't need to live in the shadow of you, Nancy.'

'I'm all confused,' I said.

'I'm doing them good, Nancy. And I'm doing you good, too. I'm turning you into a real woman. I'm giving you the chance to do what every woman on earth ought to do for a man.'

He turned to me again and said:

'I loves you, Nancy.'

'Do you, Winston?'

'Oh yes.'

'Really, really, really?'

'Yes. Really, really, really.'

'But why?' I said. 'Why? We have absolutely nothing in common. I'm not like one of your bits of fluff. I'm a mature woman. I'm older than you. I was educated at a private school on the South Coast. I know more than you.'

'Do you, Nancy?'

'Yes.'

He lay silent for a while and then he said quite suddenly:

'What's the capital of Peru?'

'What?' I said.

'What is the capital of Peru?'

'Ecuador.'

'No, Nancy, Ecuador is a country and its capital is Quito. I'll try you again. What is the longest river in the geographical entity what is known as the British Isles?'

'The Shannon.'

'Correct.'

'You see, you see,' I cried with triumph. 'I told you I was well educated.'

Winston propped himself up on one elbow and looked down on me.

'Who wrote – who was the author of *Darkness At Noon*?' he said.

'Pardon?'

'Arthur Koestler. He was the blokey what wrote *Darkness At Noon*.'

'I knew that.'

'No, you didn't.'

'I did. You never gave me the chance to answer. You bastard. You . . .'

I stopped and I took hold of his arm and whispered:

'Winston. Oh, Winston, Winston.'

He pulled my hand away gently and said:

'Hold on a mo, Nancy, and I'll just put my fag out.'

He did, but by that time I had already scampered back to my bedroom.

24

I went round in a daze next day.

The weather wasn't very nice. It was decidedly grumpy. It was fourteen degrees Celsius – that's about fifty-eight degrees Fahrenheit in real temperature.

I wondered who Fahrenheit was. Fancy discovering temperature. I wonder if his wife shopped at the greengrocers like we did.

'Pound of sprouts, Mrs Fahrenheit? Certainly, Mrs Fahrenheit. Can I interest you in satsumas today?'

I should have hated to have been Mrs Celsius. I bet he always kept her short of money and didn't aim straight when he went to the loo. That sort always do.

I went to see Father in his shed. Why I just did not know.

I pushed open the door without knocking and stepped inside and Father said:

'What ho, Nancy, old boy. Come on in. It's only me.'

'Hullo, Father,' I said. 'Are you busy?'

'Fearfully busy, old boy. I'm making sure I've got enough stocks of quinine.'

'Oh,' I said. 'And have you?'

'No. I think I'll get Winston to nip round to Timothy White and Taylor's to get me a jar. I wonder if they still sell book tokens there?'

'What?'

'Well, I'll need to read books when I'm in India, Nancy,' said Father, trying to kick an empty bottle of gin under his old creaking rocking chair. 'I'll need oodles and oodles of books, old boy. I think I might go in for Jane Austen. Fearfully pleasant books she wrote when she was alive. All about families.'

Then he chuckled and said:

'Isn't family life sheer hell?'

I went to visit Rosie in her work room, her studio.

It was quite bare and Rosie was staring out of the window, her hands clasped loosely together behind her back.

She turned when I came in, smiled her lovely, glowing smile and said:

'Hullo, Nancy.'

'Hullo, Rosie,' I said. 'All packed up, are you?'

'Yes.'

'When are you leaving?'

'At the end of the week.'

I nodded. I didn't really know what to say.

'Have you somewhere to stay?' I said.

'Not yet.'

'Oh.'

She paused. She hesitated and then she said with her eyes all soft and her voice all tremulous and shaky:

'Nance?'

And eagerly I said:

'Yes, Rosie, yes?'

And she just shrugged her shoulders and said:

'Oh never mind. It doesn't matter.'

I went to see William in his study.

He was pounding away at his typewriter. The ball bearings were rattling in the pocket of his oatmeal cardigan and he was hunchbacked and cross-kneed and frowning with concentration.

He didn't hear me enter the room, but when he turned and saw me, his face broke into a friendly grin just like the dial on the front of the central heating boiler.

'Hullo, Nancy,' he said. 'Just finishing off my monograph on the Manchester, South Junction and Altrincham Railway before I go.'

'I see,' I said. 'And is it going well?'

'Oh yes. I think I'm on the point of a major breakthrough.'

'Are you really, William? How lovely for you.'

'Isn't it?' he said and he rubbed his hands together like a silly little squirrel on the top of a swaying sycamore. 'You see, Nancy, you see, for years and years there's been this mystery surrounding the design of the bridge they used at Dane Road station at Sale Moor. Well, I've delved into the records and I've discovered the bridge at Timperley and the underpass at Warwick Road were, in fact, designed by . . .'

I crept away before he could reveal to me the solution of the mystery.

I visited Winston in the kitchen. He was baking the most scrumptious-looking Danish raspberry shortcake – at least that's what it looked like to my untutored eyes.

'Hullo, Nancy,' he said. 'What do you reckon?'

'Not a lot,' I said.

He clucked his tongue, drew breath in deeply through the blue-chipped gap in his two front teeth and said quietly:

'What's the capital of Chile?'

'Santiago,' I said.

'Correct. Who wrote the book *The Go-Between*?'

'L. P. Hartley.'

'Correct. What is the home ground of Oldham Athletic?'

'Boundary Park.'

'Correct,' said Winston and he grinned from grubby ear to grubby ear and said: 'You see, Nancy, you see. You got them all right and correct. You're learning, my old wingsy bash. At long last you're learning.'

I went to my sewing room.

I doodled with a bobbin.

Somehow I wasn't in the mood for bobbins.

I watched a butterfly fluttering at the window pane, falling on to the sill and flapping its wings and getting tangled up in the curtains.

But I wasn't in the mood for butterflies.

And then suddenly it came to me in a flash – I knew what to do.

Good grief, it was staring me in the face.

The answer to all our problems.

It was so simple.

I laughed out loud. I hugged myself. The cares slipped off me like water cascading off . . . well, never mind about that.

My spirits soared. I felt like I did all those years ago when Felicity Atkins fell off her bicycle and got gravel embedded in her nose. I was triumphant.

I resolved to tell them all at dinner.

I waited patiently all through the meal.

There was not the slightest need to rush.

Winston had cooked a superlative dinner – salmon mousse, pot roast of lamb, braised celery, purée of swede, creamed potatoes, followed by Danish raspberry shortcake and a selection of cheeses.

I listened contentedly to the chatter of the family.

'I say, Winston, old boy,' said Father. 'Yum, yum – this is the finest piece of beef I've tasted for years and years.'

'It's lamb,' said Winston.

'Is it by Jove?' said Father. 'Well, all I can say is, good on it, well done. I do like a piece of meat that knows its own mind.'

Rosie, her blonde hair all sparkly with glittery fripperies, said:

'Winston, how on earth did you get these potatoes so silky and so smooth and so creamy?'

'Simple, Rosie,' said Winston. 'I give them a thorough good pounding in the left boot of my wellies, didn't I?'

Rosie tittered and William looked up from his gorging plate and said:

'This meal is wonderful, Winston. You must give me the recipe for it when I go to London? Is it cooked or did it come from a packet?'

They chattered on and presently I banged my fork against the side of my wine glass to attract their attention.

'Well, everyone,' I said. 'I've got an announcement to make.'

'Splendid, old boy,' said Father. 'Do I need to put my glasses on?'

'It's about us,' I said.

'Us?' said Rosie.

'Yes. Us,' I said. 'I've got the answer to all our problems. Rosie wants her independence. William wants to live with her in London and have adventures. Father wants to jigger off to India.

'Well, I know how to solve it to everyone's satisfaction.

'We do what we always do.

'We move house.'

'What?' said Rosie.

I smiled broadly and I said:

129

'Simple, isn't it. We move lock, stock and barrel from here. We'll buy a house in London, and I'll be there to look after you. It'll be just like old times. You do exactly what you want to do, and there'll always be me to put you right when you go wrong.

'We'll still be together – a united, happy family.'

I faced them flushed with my triumph, bursting with pride at my victory.

'Well?' I said. 'What do you think?'

No one spoke.

'Rosie? William, Father? What do you think?'

They turned their heads away from me.

'Well?' I said. 'What do you reckon?'

There was silence.

And then Rosie said:

'Nancy.'

'Yes, Rosie?' I said eagerly. 'Yes?'

She shrugged her shoulders and said:

'Oh never mind. It doesn't matter.'

'What do you mean – never mind, it doesn't matter?' I cried. 'I've given you the chance to turn over a new leaf and lead new lives and ... and ...'

My voice tailed away. I searched for their eyes, but they turned away from me.

'Isn't anyone going to speak?' I said.

It was Winston who spoke.

He said:

'What is the capital of Venezuela?'

'I don't know,' I said.

'On which river would you find the city of Lancaster?'

'I don't know,' I said.

And very slowly I got up from the table. They didn't look at me. They hung their heads. I went into my sewing room. I looked at myself in the mirror. There was only one thing to say.

'Hullo, Nancy,' I said. 'What do you reckon? Not a lot.'

And then I shouted at the top of my voice with real, lashing venom:

'Lancaster is on the Lune, you bastard.'

25

I once saw a programme on television about the giant octopus.

After what they called 'the holocaust of procreation' – what a ghastly, horrific expression – the female of the species died.

Just like that. She kicked the bucket.

After she'd mated with the gentleman giant octopus – and that was quite a business, I can tell you, what with the writhing and the fumbling and all those disgusting sperm things – she gave birth to millions of eggs.

She stuck them to the roof of her cave deep underwater and for six months she spent her entire time fanning them with her tentacles, stroking them, caressing them, pampering and cosseting them and squirting fresh water over them so they wouldn't be eaten by algae.

She didn't go out. She didn't feed.

When the eggs hatched and turned into plankton and blithely floated away into the great yonder without so much as a by-your-leave, ungrateful little swine, she was so exhausted, so drained, so weary, she curled up and died.

Just like that. She kicked the bucket.

They showed a picture of her dying on the sea bed. It was awful. I wanted to weep.

She'd turned white. She was buffeted helplessly in the currents. Her skin flaked away in great mouldering patches from her arms. In her eyes was the desolation of endless loneliness and betrayal. And, as she lay dying, small fish nibbled at the living flesh of her limbs.

I felt just like that as I sat in the drawing room with Father.

I wanted to weep.

The mellow autumn shadows stretched lazily over the lawn like a great slothful black Labrador dog. The golden leaves on the massing beeches in the grounds of Florey Palace refused to die. The swallows hunted the long, lingering booty of summer.

I wanted to weep.

'Don't cry, Nancy,' said Father.

'I'm not crying.'

'I want you to be happy, old boy.'

'I've told you, Father – I'm not crying.'

'It's a time for rejoicing, Nancy. Not crying,' said Father, shaking the sour sluck from his pipe over the Chinese rug. 'I'm going back to India. I'm returning to the land which gave me the happiest times in the whole of my life.'

'I know, Father.'

'Then why are you crying?'

I couldn't help it. I turned from the window and blurted out:

'For God's sake, you stupid old man, I am not crying.'

Father chuckled and stuffed a sodden, clinkered pipe cleaner deep into the stem of his pipe.

'Course you're not crying,' he said. 'You're really happy for me, aren't you?'

'Oh yes, Father,' I said. 'As always. As usual.'

Father began to fill his pipe, spilling tobacco all over the knees of his white ducks, and as he hummed softly to himself he said:

'Do you know, old boy, I can feel India now crooning to me in my bones, throbbing and pulsing through my veins.'

'Oh, terrific, Father,' I said icily. 'I'm so pleased for you.'

Father lit his pipe. He puffed in vigorously and tamped down the loose tobacco with the ball of his thumb. A burning spark floated on to the lapel of his old ARP tunic top and began to smoulder. But I did not move. Why should I, when the skin of my past was flaking away in great mouldering patches and small fishes were nibbling at my living flesh?

'India!' said Father. 'I can already feel the nip of the crisp, sharp air of the high mountain passes. I can smell rich cinnamon and nutmeg buns in Simla. I can hear the slow, complaining grunt of water buffalo.

'I can see the women returning from the well, pitchers of water balanced on their heads, and their hips swaying, and their slim, smooth arms held out to balance themselves, and their limp, languid wrists rich with promise for the night to come.'

'Is that so, Father?' I said and I felt myself drifting in the heedless currents and, God save me, all I wanted to do in the world at that moment was squirt great clouds of ink over that selfish, cruel, callous old man with his smouldering tunic top and his tobacco-stained white ducks.

'India!' he said. 'I once took a ferry across the Ganges. Or was it the Indus? I don't suppose it matters all that much really. They're both fearfully riparian, aren't they?'

'Oh yes, Father,' I said. 'Without a doubt.'

'It was a dark night. No moon. Big, plump-arsed clouds and your mother was talking to this wallah with the most frightful speech impediment. I think he was a circuit judge.'

'No, Father, he was a surgeon general.'

'So he was, Nancy, so he was. Anyway, there we were drinking our pink gins when all of a sudden there was this ghastly grinding crash, and the whole boat juddered and then it started to buck and bounce and very slowly it began to list to port – or was it starboard? – and all the women started to scream and great billowing sparks shot out of the funnel and set the canvas awnings alight and . . .'

An army helicopter drowned his words. It tattered and snagged the silence, ripping at its guts, tearing it to shreds.

When it had passed by and cuckered to itself in the far distance, Father said:

'I shall miss those helicopters, when I go back to India. I really don't know how I'll manage to cope without them.'

'Oh, Father,' I said, and in an instant I forgot about the poor blind white abandoned hulk buffeted by the heedless currents. 'Oh, Father, my love, what are we going to do with you?'

'Do with me, old boy?' he said. 'There's nothing for you to do. I'm going to India. Isn't that marvellous?'

Then he paused, scratched the side of his nose with the stem of his pipe and said:

'I wonder if it's still there after all these years.'

26

What a mess!

The happy family!

Rosie was going to London. William was going to London. Father was going to ... well, goodness knows where Father was going to.

I knew I was in danger of harping on. That's what spinster ladies of a certain age do – they harp on and on.

Lost loves, the price of sprouts, starfish in the rockpools of childhood, one-man buses, sardine tins without keys, air force pilots with the flashes of 'Newfoundland' on their shoulders, Rudge bicycles with clanking chain-guards, queues at the supermarket check-out, dress shops that make you feel eighty, computerized gas bills, the whingeing diphthongs of the young, slovenliness, impoliteness, people riding their bikes on the pavements, comfy cars with running boards and leather upholstery, wrinkles, grey hairs, lost loves, long, long lost loves – on and on they harp.

I wanted to stop it. But I couldn't.

The end of the family. Total collapse.

I'd spent the whole of my life dedicating myself to keeping us together. What a farce. We were splitting up. I'd failed completely.

What had been the point of it all?

All the washing and the ironing and the shopping and the endless, mindless drudgery. All those laxatives on Friday nights. All the tears, all the tantrums, all the bitter arguments and the hurtful, wounding words.

And what was it that hurt me most? When I said we'd all move back to London and I'd care for them and look after them, pamper them, bully them, let them lead lives of total independence – within reason, of course – and what did they do?

They turned their backs on me and rejected me.

Out of hand. And why?

Because of Winston.

I didn't want to harp on about it, but . . .

Winston! Bloody Winston. They worshipped him and they hadn't the faintest idea of what he'd done to them.

Bastard!

They thought he'd released them, liberated them and it was all in their interest and their interests alone.

Rot! Rubbish! Poppycock.

What they didn't know was . . .

I tried hard not to. I really did. I tried desperately not to harp on about it, but it was no use.

I resolved to tell them. I'd tell them what Winston had really been up to.

I'd gather them for a family conference and I'd say:

'You've been taken in, you poor, hopeless boobies, you pathetic load of chumps. Winston wants to boot you out of the house so he can be alone with me.'

The presumption of it!

Me. Nancy. A mature woman. Privately educated. I'd seen Sir Geraint Evans personally in the flesh. I'd been shopping in the Koenigs-alle in Dortmund. If I hadn't had chicken pox at the crucial moment, I'd have travelled first class on the Golden Arrow.

What did I want with a nauseating village Romeo with his bits of fluff on the side and his flubbery belly and his . . .

I decided to take the bull by the horns immediately. Very calmly and very rationally I would tell them the truth.

I would, of course, dress myself appropriately and change into something rather severe.

I stowed away the hoover in his cupboard under the stairs and went upstairs to the bedroom to prepare myself for the confrontation.

*

And as Nancy Empson was preparing her wardrobe Rosie and William were having their own confrontation in the drawing room.

'Why can't I live with you in London, Rosie?' said William.

'Because I don't want you to, William.'

'Why?'

'Because I want to live on my own.'

'Why?'

'Because, William, I am sick and tired of this family. I hate it. I'm fed up to the back teeth with it. And so I intend to change my whole life. I intend to be placid and good-natured. Happy smile. Sparkling eyes.

'I intend to laugh a lot. I've been practising and I've discovered I rather like laughing. It's good fun.

'But with you living with me, William, all I would do is scream my head off.'

'Maybe,' said William. 'But why can't I just share with you till I find somewhere of my own?'

'No, William. No, no, no.'

I was only halfway down the stairs when I could hear them screaming at each other.

I was wearing the smart, black cocktail dress I'd bought for the RSPCA annual dinner-dance when we lived in Shrewsbury all those years ago. I was wearing black patent leather court shoes and a thin string of cultured pearls. I was going to wear my diamanté clip-on earrings, but I couldn't find them. Not to worry, they always made my lobes throb when I got agitated.

I paused for a moment outside the drawing room, the sitting room, breathed in deeply and composed myself.

Then I threw open the door, and I said:

'I see. Screaming again, are we?'

'Yes, Nancy, yes,' said Rosie. 'But not for long. This is the last outburst. I'd make the most of it, if I were you. From now on there's going to be a new Rosie – placid, gentle, tranquil and serene.'

I snorted scornfully and said:

'Never mind that. I've something important to tell you.'

Rosie groaned and William said:

'Oh no, not again?'

Before I could respond, however, Winston entered the room.

He smiled at us and said:

'Ah. All gathered together, are we? Sorry if I'm butting in look.'

'What do you want?' I snapped at him.

'I got something to tell you,' said Winston. 'And I needs you to be calm.'

'We're always calm,' said Rosie.

'Course you are, Rosie,' said Winston. 'That's why I don't wants you flying off the handle.'

'Well, go on then, man,' I said testily. 'Spit it out.'

Winston nodded and sucked in through the blue-chipped gap in his two front teeth.

Then he said:

'It's your father. He's conked out in his shed.'

27

I went cold.

Ghastly visions flashed across my mind.

Father impaled through the chest with a rusty garden fork. Father lying bloodied and shredded in a pile of empty gin bottles. Father gored by a water buffalo. Father incinerated in a blazing ARP tunic top. Father clinging to the spars of a sinking Indian ferry, screaming for help. Screaming, screaming, screaming.

But it was Rosie who was screaming.

'Oh my God. Oh my God. I knew it. I knew it would happen sooner or later. And it's all your fault, Nancy. You've been badgering him and bullying him . . .'

'Shut up,' said Winston in a firm and infinitely masterful voice. 'I don't want no panics. I don't want no hysterics.'

'I'm not being hysterical,' screamed Rosie.

At this Winston bellowed:

'Shut up. Shut your bleeding trap.'

Instantly Rosie fell silent, and Winston turned to me with a gentle smile and said in a voice just like Richard Todd in *The Dam Busters*:

'Nancy, I wants you to go to the telephone, at once sort of thing, and ring for the doctor. And then you're to put four pillows on your father's bed and get him a clean po.'

'Yes, Winston,' I said. 'I'll do it straightaway.'

He turned to Rosie and said:

'Rosie.'

'Yes, Winston?'

'You're to go into the kitchen and make a pot of strong tea.'

'Yes, Winston. Right away.'

'And, Rosie.'

'Yes, Winston?'

'No hysterics. No tantrums.'

'No, Winston.'

William put his hand up and said:

'Excuse me. Can I be of any assistance?'

'Yes, you can, my old pile of hedgehog turd,' said Winston. 'You're to go to the drinks tray and pour out a very large and very stiff glass of brandy.'

'But Father doesn't like brandy, Winston.'

'It ain't for him, pillock,' said Winston. 'It's for me.'

Rosie flared up again and shouted:

'How dare you drink brandy at a time like this? How dare you . . .'

Winston gave her one of his looks, noble, manly, severe and virile and potent and said:

'Rosie.'

'Yes, Winston?'

'The tea.'

'Yes, Winston.'

'And don't forget to warm the bleeding pot look.'

We did as we were told. And Winston went to the shed and carried Father in his arms upstairs and very gently laid him in his bed and propped up the pillows behind his head.

Father groaned.

His face was yellow with white blotches round his eyes, and his lips were sheened with blue. His legs twitched, and he held his head at a most curious angle.

I went cold again.

Talk about chickens coming home to roost. I'd killed Father before. In the River Florey. Drowned him. Well, not literally. He'd lingered on a bit. But then he died and we had a funeral. Not literally. It was all in my imagination. But it was the thought that counted.

Rosie stood by the side of his bed, snivelling.

'He's dying,' she said. 'I know it – he's dying.'

'Rosie,' said Winston.

'Yes, Winston?'

'Pour out the tea.'

'Yes, Winston.'

The doctor came. He smelled most peculiar. He had bloodshot eyes and an enormous, obscene, purple pustule on the corner of his mouth. He was in the room for ages and ages.

I clung to Winston's arm tightly.

He stroked my hair tenderly and said:

'There, there, Nancy. There ain't nothing to worry your arse about.'

'No?' I said.

'No,' said Winston. 'He's shit hot as a doctor, is Doctor Betmead. He used to play second row forward for Gloucester till his piles got too bad. He's been in at the birth of every one of my countless sprogs and apart from them all being as ugly as sin I ain't never ever had one word of complaint against him.'

'Yes, Winston, I'm sure you haven't,' I said. 'But it might have escaped your notice that this is not a case of childbirth. Good grief, man, this is a case of . . .'

'Nancy.'

'Yes, Winston?'

'No panics. No tantrums.'

'No, Winston.'

William appeared with a large glass on the silver salver Father had found in the attic of the house in Oakham, Rutlandshire, all those years ago.

'Here's the brandy, Winston,' he said.

'Good man, William,' said Winston.

'Only it's not brandy,' said William, looking decidedly flushed and flustered. 'It's whisky. I made a mistake, you see. In my panic I poured out a glass of whisky. So I drank it myself intending to repair my error and pour out a glass of brandy. Only I didn't. I poured out another glass of whisky and . . .'

'William!'

'Yes, Winston?'

'Give it here.'

'Certainly, Winston.'

141

He handed the glass to Winston who knocked back its contents in a single gulp.

He smiled, passed the empty glass to William and said:

'I think a glass of rum would go down a treat now.'

'Certainly, Winston.'

The doctor took us downstairs to the sitting room. He hitched up his golf socks, adjusted his binocular case, drank a rather stiff whisky and soda and told us that Father's life was drawing peacefully to a close.

He was tired.

His heart was old.

He was in no pain.

He was quite serene.

We gave the doctor another whisky – an exceptionally stiff one, I thought, considering it was a beer tumbler with a chipped edge – and then we helped him to his car, fastened his seat belt for him and waved him goodbye.

He crashed his gears twice.

And then we set off for Father's bedroom.

'I don't think I'll come with you, Nancy,' said Winston.

'Why ever not?' I said.

Winston shuffled his feet and rubbed his arms and swayed from side to side.

'Well, you don't want me, missus. You don't want old Winston sort of thing. This is family business look.'

'Of course it is, Winston,' I said, clutching hold of his arm. 'And that's why we want you. That's why we need you. You are family now, Winston. You're part of the family.'

'Thank you, Nancy,' said Winston. 'I'm much obliged. I'm very touched. And that being the case, I shall come with you and accompany you with the greatest pleasure. And, William.'

'Yes, Winston?'

'When you goes into your father's bedroom, I don't want you rattling your ball bearings and picking your nose with your tiepin.'

'Certainly, Winston.'

'And, Rosie.'

'Yes, Winston?'

'You smile and be tender and gentle – and no bleeding rows. Do I make myself clear?'

'Yes, Winston.'

We went upstairs to Father's bedroom. We settled ourselves round his bed.

He didn't speak.

I looked round their faces, and, do you know, I felt happy.

Yes, I felt deliriously happy.

I couldn't help it, but I felt happy and contented.

The family was together once more. The family would remain together. And I wasn't a failure. And my life hadn't been in vain. And I didn't feel a moment's guilt thinking such thoughts.

There was a movement from the bed. Father was waving his left hand feebly and clutching at his throat.

We didn't move.

We didn't know what to do.

Presently he spoke.

'Nancy,' he said.

'Yes, Father,' I said.

'Are you there, Nancy?'

At this I saw red. I really did.

'But, of course, I'm here, Father. Good grief, man, I'm . . .'

I was stopped by Winston.

'Nancy!' he said sharply.

'Sorry, Winston, sorry,' I said. And I felt so ashamed, I felt so humiliated.

I leaned forwards to Father and I said gently:

'We're all here, Father. Rosie, William, Winston, me. We're all here.'

'Whacko. Jolly Dee. Fearfully pleasant of you,' said Father.

A faint smile came to his face. He licked his lips and then after a while he said:

'I've a confession to make.'

'Now, Father, don't upset yourself,' said Rosie. 'Just lie still.'

'I am lying still,' said Father. 'I'm lying very still. It's my legs, you see. The old pins. They seem to belong to someone else. I think they belong to that Sikh chartered accountant I once met in Bombay. Or was it Amritsar?'

'Amritsar, Father,' said William. 'It was Amritsar.'

'Quite right, William. So it was,' said Father. 'I met him in Bombay.'

He dozed off for a while.

I looked round his bedroom.

It was gloomy and it smelled of hollow chests and threadbare knees. Under the window was an old tin cabin trunk, battered and covered with faded, peeling travel labels. Above the fireplace was the head of a leopard with one eye missing and scorch marks on its snout. The picture of Mother glared down at us from the dressing table. She was wearing a Bavarian trilby hat and she was standing next to Henry Cotton.

And then very slowly Father struggled to haul himself upright from his pillows. Rosie moved to help him, but Winston stopped her with a sharp hiss through the gap in his two front teeth. At length Father installed himself on his right elbow, his left arm hanging loosely over the side of the bed. He panted for a few moments, and then he opened his eyes, smiled and said:

'I've never been to India, you know.'

'What?' said Winston.

Father giggled.

He flapped vaguely with his left arm and his shoulders heaved in silent mirth.

'Yes, I've never been to India,' he said. 'Never set foot in the place. I've been to Scotland. I've been to Lithuania. And Estonia. But I've never been to India.'

Should I? Or should I not?

I looked across to Winston. His eyes were wide open with astonishment and he had his left hand inside his shirt furiously scratching his armpit.

Rosie had her head averted. And William was fiddling with the hem of his oatmeal cardigan.

And then I said it. I could not do otherwise.

'We know, Father,' I said. 'We always have known.'

'Yes, Nancy, yes,' said Father. 'I know it must come as a fearful shock to you, my not having been to India. It's come as a great shock to me, old boy.

'I should have been an Indian Office man, you now. Oodles and oodles of gin. Pig sticking. Shooting tigers. Going for treks in the Himalayas. Learning the dialects of the remote hill tribes. Playing footer with the chaps from the regiment. Being unfaithful to your mother with Mrs Ventris.'

'Who's Mrs Ventris, Father?' said Rosie.

'Mrs Ventris ran a sweetshop in Macclesfield. Or was it Minehead?' said Father. 'I don't suppose it matters really.

'She rode a sit-up-and-beg bicycle, Mrs Ventris, and every time she saw me she used to ring her bell like billio. Fearfully merry, I thought. Fearfully merry of her. I like merry women.'

'Of course you do, Father,' said Rosie.

'Your mother wasn't a merry woman.'

'We know, Father,' I said.

'She was a very discontented woman, your mother. Exceedingly discontented,' said Father. 'I remember one day we were playing gin rummy in the rest bungalow in the Naga Hills. Or was it the Punjab? I don't suppose it matters really. But, anyway, we were . . . we were . . . I've never been to India, you know. Never never in the whole of my life.'

'We know, Father,' said William. 'We've always known. And that's why we've loved you so much. They were such wonderful stories. Oodles and oodles better than my silly stories about the Lancashire and North Western Railway.'

'Of course they were. It's because they were true,' said Father and then slowly he slid back down his pillows and closed his eyes. We looked on silently.

'Never been to India. Never never,' he mumbled. 'And I'll tell you something else, too.'

'What's that, Father?' said Rosie.

'I've never been to Lithuania. Or was it Macclesfield?'

After a while he nodded off.

William and Rosie crept out silently to make some lunch. Winston and I sat together at the foot of the bed, and he took hold of my hand and whispered:

'Nancy.'

'Yes, Winston?'

'I loves you, Nancy. I desires you and I wants you.'

'Winston, oh, Winston,' I whispered.
And a smile came to Father's face. He smiled.
And he grunted with contentment.

28

Whilst Nancy Empson and Winston were keeping their vigil in Father's bedroom, William and Rosie sat in the kitchen.

'What's going on up there?' said William. 'Why haven't they come down for lunch?'

'They're keeping watch, William,' said Rosie. 'Like a pair of shy and awkward shepherds in a school nativity play.'

'Nancy looks so happy,' said William.

'Mm.'

'So does Winston.'

'Mm.'

William spread a helping of Winston's chutney and asparagus dip over his cream cracker and said:

'I suppose this is the end of it all now.'

'Yes, William, I suppose it is. Poor Father. All his stories about India. All his secret drinking we weren't supposed to know about. All his army helicopters and seeing Ranji score a ton at Maidstone or was it Canterbury?'

'Canterbury.'

'It's all gone for him now. It's the end.'

William took another cream cracker from the barrel and spread it with Winston's home-potted meat paste and said:

'I wasn't talking about that end, Rosie. I was talking about the end of our plans to move to London.'

Rosie's nostrils flared and her eyes flashed.

'End of our plans? What the hell are you talking about, William?' she snarled.

Then she composed herself and said:

'No, Rosie. Be calm. Be placid. Be tranquil and serene. Right?'

She leaned across the table and patted William gently on the hand.

'William, my sweetheart, this is not the end of our plans,' she said. 'We are still going to London. At least I'm still going to London.'

'But what about Father? You can't leave him like this.'

'I shall wait for Father to die,' said Rosie. 'I shall attend his funeral. I shall weep for him. I shall weep for our past life – all those moves from house to house, all those packing cases bursting with books, all that crockery wrapped in crumpled newspaper, all those removal men and their cups of tea and their flirtatious leers, all those ... How curious. All I remember of our past life is moving from house to house.

'Well, I shall kiss it all a fond goodbye, William. And then I shall set up a new life for myself. Just me. Just Rosie. Whacko. Jolly Dee – a life dedicated just to me.'

And then she turned her head away from her brother and said softly:

'Or will I? Will I ever do it?'

Father drifted on.

The doctor said he was in no pain. He said he was peaceful. He gave us the first two winners at Kempton Park.

We took it in turn to sit at Father's bedside.

We were united as a family.

And I was happy.

It was lovely sitting there in that gloomy old bedroom with Father's spats hanging all forlorn from a peg behind the door and letting my thoughts take flight.

All those ambitions. All those dreams. But there was no bitterness, no resentment. I could look at them calmly and smile wryly from time to time and giggle to myself.

I always wanted to be an air hostess.

I'd loved to have been an air hostess on one of those snow-white Empire flying boats. When we lived in the Medway Valley all those years ago we used to see them moored on the river at Rochester. Or was it Chatham? It doesn't matter really.

How marvellous to fly over the Nile Delta serving caviare and scrambled eggs to planters returning to Kenya and their farms in the cool, green mountains with the lakes shimmering in the dusk with the pink glow of roosting flamingos.

How wonderful to sit in the cockpit with the pilot as we swooped low over South Sea atolls and landed smooth as a swan on the surface of a coral lagoon. And in the evening we'd go to dinner, the pilot and I, to a thatched inn with a verandah open to the tropic stars and there'd be fat Dutchmen with sun-blotched necks smoking stubby cigars and drinking schnapps and there'd be thin, shy Assistant District Commissioners in baggy shorts and pith helmets down to their ears ogling me and staring at my ankles and the pilot would pat my knee under the table and play footsie and tell me about his daughter who was struck dead with polio at the age of five and a half.

When we lived in Styal, Cheshire, all those years ago there was an air hostess staying next door with her uncle. Stuck-up cow. She was fifty if she was a day and I know for a fact she never flew farther than the Isle of Man.

All those dreams. All those ambitions.

It would have been lovely to have married Prince Philip, if you didn't mind him being away from home all the time slaughtering partridges.

I would have made a terrific Chief Guide. For a start off I'd have changed the uniform of those ghastly Sea Rangers with their thick ankles and their pebble-dashed spectacles. I'd have had them like a shot in French camiknickers, black velvet chokers and flashing lights on the tips of their berdongers.

I could have been a farmer's wife in the Lake District and served cream teas to the hikers and written humorous short stories in the local dialect for *The Dalesman* and become a Justice of the Peace and sent all those ghastly flashers from Leeds to lengthy terms in prison and in the fullness of time fallen in love with a university lecturer stranded by the snows in winter and run away with him to Exeter University and borne him a daughter who'd become chief flautist with the Suisse Romande Symphony Orchestra in Geneva. Or was it Zurich? I don't suppose it matters really.

All those memories.

Being sick in the lift at Kendal Milne's in Manchester. Widdling on

Father Christmas's knee in Scholfields in Leeds. Having my first period in the ladies loo at Cockaynes in Sheffield and being so lonely and so afraid and so ashamed. My panties dropping to my ankles in the food hall at Bentalls in Kingston-upon-Thames.

Lovely, lovely memories.

And Father lingered on.

Mostly he slept.

But sometimes he would twitch his left leg, open his eyes and smile.

One morning we were all gathered round his bed and Rosie was soothing his brow with a damp face cloth, when he opened his eyes and said:

'You're just like your mother, Nancy.'

'It's not Nancy, Father. It's me – Rosie.'

'So you are. And you're just like your mother. She was never satisfied with life, your mother.'

'Wasn't she, Father?' said Rosie, gently stroking his cheek.

'No, Nancy, no.'

'It's not Nancy, Father. It's me – Rosie.'

'Same thing, old boy, same thing,' said Father.

He closed his eyes again and dozed for ten or so minutes.

Then he said:

'Your mother always used to say to me: "Why aren't you this?" Or "Why aren't you that?" Fearfully dissatisfied with her lot, your mother.'

'Now then, Father, don't upset yourself,' said Rosie.

'I'm not, Nancy, I'm not,' he said. 'Your mother used to listen to the wireless on the BBC and she'd turn to me and say: "Why can't you be Our Economics Correspondent?" Or "Why aren't you the question master on Round Britain Quiz?" Or "Why can't you be W. Barrington Dalby?" Or was it Jean Metcalfe? I don't suppose it matters really. They'd both got loud voices.'

The days passed. The autumn would not give in to winter. Why should it? It wasn't yet time.

We sat by Father's bedside.

William and Rosie did the day shift.

Winston and I spent the nights with him.

Once he woke up and said in a very loud voice:

'Pantaloons.'

On another night when the hedgehogs snuffled and starlings stamped n the eaves, he woke up and said in a soft, reedy voice:

'Hammer toes. I wonder if Goering had hammer toes.'

He fell asleep again.

And Winston felt for my hand in the darkness, took hold of it tightly and said:

'Nancy.'

'Yes, Winston?'

'It's just you and me together now, ain't it, Nancy?'

'Yes, Winston. I suppose it is.'

'Are you happy, Nancy?'

I paused for a moment and then I said:

'Yes, Winston. I suppose I am.'

'I got such plans for us, Nancy.'

'Have you, Winston?'

'Oh yes, that I has without a shadow of a doubt. When your old dad snuffs it, kicks the bucket sort of thing, we'll . . .'

'Winston!' I hissed.

'Shush, Nancy. Not so loud.'

I put my mouth close to his ear and whispered fiercely:

'We can't talk like that in front of Father when he's dying on his death bed.'

'Then we'll go outside look. We'll go into the garden and we'll talk there.'

'Yes, but . . .'

'We'll go into the garden, Nancy,' said Winston firmly.

We went into the garden.

It was restful but wary. It was peaceful but alert.

The moon shone.

I thought of clove-scented walled gardens under a sickled Arab moon. I thought of wicked, whispering gardens in the chateaux of the Loire and the rustle of silk and soft, stifled sighs of ecstasy. I thought of the terraced garden in Bowdon, Cheshire, and ice clinking in the glasses of Pimms Number One and night skulking and leering in the darkling rhododendrons and the second team wicket keeper pressing me to the ground next to the goldfish pond and me sitting on his spectacles.

Winston sighed deeply and said:

'Perfection, Nancy. Sheer perfection.'

'Oh yes, Winston,' I said hoarsely. 'Yes, yes.'

'Just perfect for a good long secret slosher, eh?'

I hit him sharply on the chest and said:

'Winston, what a dreadful thing to say.'

But I couldn't stop my giggle.

We sat side by side on the stone bench in the rose arbour and he took hold of my hand again and said:

'I got such plans for you and me, Nancy.'

'But what about your wife, Winston? What about your children?'

'The ankle-biters? The missus?' said Winston. 'Oh, don't you bother about them, Nancy. Old Winston's took care of all that.'

'But how?'

'I've told them to bugger off.'

'Winston!'

'My wife, my missus look, she is without a doubt the ugliest woman what I ever met in the whole of my born days. And so are my sprogs. Well then, I went round to see her last night and I put it to her straight. I says: "You are an ugly woman. You has nine ugly sprogs. And now you has an ugly fancy man. Well then, you're in clover, ain't you?"'

'And what did she say?'

'She said, Nancy, she said: "You're a philosopher, Winston. Can I keep your car, your motor?" And I said: "Without a doubt, my old wingsy bash, without a shadow of a doubt."'

'And what happened?'

'We shook hands, Nancy. We agreed to part all amicable sort of thing. And so here I am, missus, at your disposal.'

'Winston, I don't know what to say.'

Winston chuckled.

'We're in clover now, Nancy. Rosie's going. William's going. Your old dad's going. So there's just you left, Nancy. Just you. On your tod. On your Jack. Except for one important thing – me. Old Winston.'

It was just like the top blowing out from a bottle of well-shaken cream soda. Bang. It exploded. And before I could stop it, out it flooded.

'Oh, Winston, Winston, I've got such plans for us.'

'You got plans, Nancy? You got plans for us?'

'Of course I have. When they go, we'll start a new life. We'll move from here. We'll go and live somewhere nice. We'll live near the shops. You can enrol in the Open University and we'll go to Florence for our holidays. I've been to Florence three times, Winston.'

'Have you, Nancy? Have you now?'

'Yes. It's wonderful, Winston. It's so stimulating. I'll show you the Prado Gallery and . . .'

'He's in Madrid, Nancy.'

'What?'

'The Prado Gallery – he's in Madrid, Nancy. It's the Uffizi what's in Florence look.'

'Oh,' I said. 'My mistake. Anyway, Winston, I'll make a new man of you. I'll educate you. I'll open up new horizons in your life. We'll live somewhere nice with a red Aga cooker and a basement flat we can let off for students. And we'll go to symphony concerts and celebrity lectures and . . .'

'And bed.'

'What?'

Winston moved closer to me in the darkness and put his arm round my waist. I love having a man's arm round my waist. It's so much nicer than having his penknife digging into you.

Winston whispered softly:

'Shall we go to bed, Nancy? You and me. A nice large warm, loving, heaving bed sort of thing. Shall we share that together, my old wingsy bash?'

I felt myself go all trembly.

How I'd always longed to share a bed with a man on a regular basis. How wonderful to wipe up the crumbs when he's had cream crackers and processed cheese in bed. How marvellous to fold up his pyjamas and lay them neatly under the pillow after he's dropped them on the floor. How sumptuous and delectable to put your hand out in the middle of the night and feel the echoes of his warmth while he's in the loo having a nocturnal tinkle.

I took hold of his hand and pressed it to my tummy.

'Yes, Winston,' I said. 'Yes, I suppose sharing a bed together would be the nicest of all.'

153

'Then you'd best tell Rosie and William.'

'What?' I said.

'Tomorrow,' said Winston. 'You tell Rosie and William what you just told me now.'

'But they're going already, Winston. Why should they need to know?'

'Tomorrow,' said Winston. 'You tell them.'

Oh, how firm he was.

I longed with all my heart that he would be equally firm in bed.

29

The following day I invited Rosie and William out to lunch.

'But what about Father?' said Rosie. 'We can't leave him on his own.'

'Winston's looking after him,' I said.

'But Winston's not family,' said William. 'What if Father should die?'

'Winston is looking after him and we are going out to lunch. Right?' I said.

And I was so firm and masterful and manly that Rosie shrugged her shoulders and said:

'Right, Nancy. Anything you say.'

I took them to this expensive restaurant I know where the army officers talked in loud voices and their wives complained about the bill.

When we had finished the meal – it was terribly expensive – I folded up my napkin neatly and said:

'I've something important to say to you.'

'Well, before you start, Nancy,' said Rosie, 'we've something important to say to you, haven't we, William?'

'Yes.'

'What is it?' I said, impatient with the interruption but determined to keep my cool, not like that ghastly army wife with the perm like a tank trap who was berating the poor little Portuguese waiter with the sad, doleful eyelids.

What he'd done to offend her, goodness alone knows. If I'd been him I'd have had her on the mat with the kebab skewers ages ago. I'd have . . .

'Well then?' I said. 'Out with it.'

'You tell her, William,' said Rosie.

William looked decidedly shifty for a moment, I thought. But then he swallowed hard, drained his wine glass and said:

'You know those plans that Rosie and I have for leaving home and moving to London?'

'Yes,' I said.

'We've changed them. We're stopping here.'

'What?'

'We're staying here,' said Rosie.

'But why?'

'Well,' said Rosie. 'Well, we've been very close this past few weeks. I don't think we've ever been so close, have we, William?'

'No.'

'Sitting by Father's bedside watching him drift and linger, listening to him talk and ramble, well, it's changed our minds. It's given us a new outlook on life, hasn't it, William?'

'Yes,' said William. 'We realize that we've both been unbearably selfish. All we've been doing is thinking of ourselves. Never once have we thought of you.'

'Me?' I said. 'Me?'

'You, Nancy,' said Rosie.

William, warming to his task, poured out the last dregs of the bottle of wine – outrageously expensive, I might add – drank it in a single gulp and continued:

'When Father dies, and we go, what will happen to you, Nancy? We'd never thought of that. It had never occurred to us. What'll happen to you? You'll be on your own. How will you cope?'

'Your whole life has been dedicated to us, Nancy,' said Rosie. 'And we've taken everything for granted.'

'We've gobbled you up,' said William, knocking over the salt cellar with his elbow as he leaned across to me. 'We've been like cannibals feasting off you. Well, it's all going to change, isn't it, Rosie?'

'Yes. We're going to stay, Nancy. I can do my designs here. I don't need to go to London. I can do my designs here just as well. Better, in fact. Now I've changed my attitude to life, they'll be infinitely better.'

'And I'll write much better books,' said William. 'I'll move into totally new fields. Forget railways. I'll go into coastal steamers.'

Rosie's eyes were glinting with happiness and sparkling with love when she said:

'So we're staying on, Nancy. We're staying with you.'

'But I don't want you,' I said.

'What?' said Rosie.

'I don't need you.'

'What?' said William.

'I've got Winston.'

'Winston?' said Rosie, and she knocked over the pepper mill.

'Yes,' I said. 'That's the important thing I was going to tell you.'

You should have seen the looks on their faces.

It was as though I'd told them I was going to hitch up my skirts, rip off my knickers and chase the little Portuguese waiter all round the restaurant, drooling and slavering. Knowing the management, they'd have probably charged me corkage.

William shook his head and grimaced.

'I don't understand,' he said.

'Winston and I are going to live together,' I said slowly and clearly. 'He's settled everything with his wife and the ankle-biters. He's going to give her his motor, his car, and we're going to live together somewhere nice and it'll be near the shops and . . .'

'You and Winston,' gasped Rosie. 'I just don't believe it.'

At this I turned to her sharply and snapped:

'Well, why not? Why not me and Winston?'

And then I lowered my eyes and said very softly:

'Why not me and Winston?'

Rosie stretched out and took my hand. She squeezed my hand. She put her fingers gently under my chin and raised it so that she was staring deep into my eyes.

'Why not, Nancy?' she said. 'Why not?'

And she began to laugh. Softly at first. But she laughed, and she looked beautiful. And William laughed. And for the first time in his life he didn't look gormless.

And I laughed.

And I ordered three large glasses of port.

Not the vintage port, because the price was absolutely out of the window.

Rosie raised her glass and said:

'Well then, Nancy. To you and Winston.'

'To you and Winston,' said William.

We clinked glasses and I said:

'And you don't mind?'

'I'm thrilled, Nancy,' said Rosie. 'I'm absolutely delighted.'

'And you'll go to London?' I said timidly.

And then I blurted out:

'You must go to London. You must, you must.'

'Yes, Nancy, we'll go to London,' said Rosie with a warm smile rilling with affection and warmth. 'And then there'll be just you and Winston. But you must promise me one thing.'

'What's that?'

'You won't make him get rid of those tattoos above his nipples.'

'I promise, Rosie,' I said. 'You never know, I might find a suitable place for another one, mightn't I?'

We drove home, and we sang in the car. We actually sang. There were no squabbles, no tantrums. And Rosie said just as we were entering the village:

'I'm so happy for you, Nancy.'

'So am I,' said William. 'I'm so happy for all of us.'

When we got home, Winston was waiting for us at the front door.

There was a look of extreme alarm on his face.

'Oh, my God, it's Father,' cried Rosie. 'Oh, my God, he's . . .'

'This way,' said Winston sternly. 'Follow me.'

My heart tumbled and plunged and looped the loop.

He was dead. Father had kicked the bucket. What on earth would I wear for the funeral? Should I invite people back to the house after or should I book the village hall? Should I . . .

Winston led us into the drawing room, the sitting room, and there was Father.

He was fully dressed in black frock coat and bottle-green plus fours.

He was sitting in the winged armchair, smoking his pipe and drinking a glass of neat gin.

'Whatho, chaps,' he said.

'Father!' I cried. 'What are you doing out of bed? You're supposed to be at death's door.'

'I know,' said Father. 'Load of old rot, isn't it?'

'Winston, what on earth is going on?' I said.

'I don't know, Nancy,' said Winston. 'I was downstairs baking a red-currant tart with dried juniper berries, when I looks up and there's your father, your old dad, standing at the door fully dressed. I bloody near shit myself, I did.'

'Frightfully amusing,' said Father.

Rosie moved towards Father and said.

'Father, the doctor specifically told you . . .'

'Never mind the quack, Rosie,' said Father. 'Fearful chap with his damp fingers and his duff racing tips. Reminds me of a quack I once knew in India. Damn fine polo player but an absolute duffer when it came to mumps.'

'Father, I just do not understand,' I said.

'It's very simple, Nancy,' he said. 'I was just tired. That's all. Very very tired. Exceedingly tired. And then I woke up, and I thought, jigger me, they think I'm going to die. What fearful rot. I'm not dying. I'm still in my prime. Still got a whole new life ahead of me. Yes, a whole new life. With the whole family.'

'What?' said William.

'What?' said Rosie.

I could not speak. The blood froze in my veins.

Father chuckled and said:

'Yes, chaps. The whole of us together. We'll stay on here and be a united family just like we always were.

'We'll have rows and tantrums and squabbles and Winston can go back home to his wife and children and come across from time to time to mend our stench pipe and repair the central heating boiler and cook us yummy yummy nosh and . . .

'You know, all this reminds me of an exceedingly quarrelsome family I once knew in Cawnpore.

'Or was it Goa?'

'No, Father,' I said. 'It was here. It was very definitely here.'

Crunch, crash – the whole of my life came tumbling down in ruins.

30

The sun was plump.

The fields were plump with pheasant. The cattle were plump in the pastures. Bullfinches, sleek-capped and bulbous of breast flashed their rumps in orchards groaning with fruit. The beeches billowed in the flanks of the Downs. The river creamed succulent and sweet against the piers of the old stone bridge.

The wind was plump from the south.

And I was thin with misery.

I was desolate.

My soul was rimed and chapped with winter frost. My brain shivered. The sockets of my eyeballs were encrusted with creaking ice.

And who cared?

Not a single sinner.

Father refused to die.

Rosie and William refused to leave the village and move to London.

And the family was happy.

You could see it in the malice in their eyes. You could hear it in the bitter pitch of their voices. Tension hovered all round the house. It hissed. It spat.

Everything was back to normal.

For breakfast that morning Winston served us devilled kidneys, creamy scrambled eggs, thick Wiltshire ham, orange segments sodden in home-made elderberry wine and . . .

Winston.

I'd such plans for him.

We'd take up ballroom dancing and buy a Newfoundland pup and call it Esme. I'd teach him golf, if he promised not to scratch his crutch whilst he was teeing off. I'd buy him a pin-stripe suit and black silk socks for when we went to the opening nights of the Amateur Light Operatics.

We wouldn't make friends unless they were nice.

We'd give the dustmen a cheery wave when they collected the rubbish and we'd read historical novels set in the Regency period.

We'd be alone. We'd be together. We'd be contented and happy.

Oh, Winston, Winston.

What had they done to you and me?

31

Nancy Empson sat alone in her sewing room among the haggard silks and cottons and the pinched, silent shrill of the walls.

And in the garden Father sat in a deck chair in his blazer and his panama, smoking his pipe and wafting his mauve and ochre silk bandana idly at the wasps.

Rosie and William watched him silently from the patio where the French marigolds blazed and glared at the sun in their plump terracotta pots.

An army helicopter sickered and sackered low overhead, smoke snarling from its exhausts, its rotors chomping back the stillness.

'I say, helicopters,' said Father. 'The ninth today. Whacko. Jolly Dee.'

He puffed contentedly at his pipe. The smoke billowed round him and then coiled away in thin whisps.

He nodded to himself and said:

'When we lived in India, your mother and I, when she was alive, we used to have mosquitoes as big as helicopters.

'Fearful blighters, they were. I remember once we were listening to the World Service on the British Broadcasting Corporation – the Palm Court Orchestra with Jack Byfield, Reginald Kilbey and Max Jaffa. Or was it Big Bill Campbell and His Rocky Mountain Rhythm? I don't suppose it matters really.

'Anyway, there we were eating mint humbugs and trying to work the fretwork machine by the light of the hurricane lamp, when all of a sudden we heard the most tremendous buzzing noise and . . .

His voice tailed off. He closed his eyes and began to doze.

'Just look at him,' said Rosie.

'Yes,' said William.

'He's indestructible, isn't he?'

'Yes.'

'He'll outlive us all, William. He'll outlive the world. When the final cataclysmic bang comes, Father will be sitting in his armchair, puffing his pipe and burning holes in the front of his cardigan and he'll say: "I say, another helicopter. Whacko. Jolly Dee." '

'Yes.'

'And I'm staying here because of him.'

'Yes.'

'Thank God for that.'

'What?'

'You idiot, William. Don't you understand? Father's recovery came in the nick of time. He was the perfect excuse.'

'Why?'

'Think about it, you pathetic little numbskull. I couldn't have coped with moving to London. My own flat. Come and go as I please. Be my own boss. No need to think of anyone but myself. Terrifying, William. I was frightened out of my wits.'

'Yes, I can imagine it, Rosie.'

'For Christ's sake, who could I quarrel with? What could I complain about? Who could I blame when things went wrong? It would be all down to me and me alone. I'd be totally responsible for myself.'

'I know.'

'I couldn't cope with the burden of being happy, William. I wouldn't know how to handle it. I need the family. I can't survive without our jealousies and our squabbles and our dissatisfaction and our bleakness. Pathetic, isn't it?'

'Not really.'

'Is that what you feel, too? Is that why you've decided to stay?'

'Partly.'

'Well, what was the main reason?'

'Winston.'

'Ah, Winston. What would we do without dear old faithful Winston in our lives?'

William nodded.

'Exactly, Rosie, exactly,' he said.

A straggle and a tatter of rooks passed silently overhead.

A jet plane slivered its white trail high over the blue dome of the sky.

And William continued:

'You know when Winston was trying to give me the courage to move to London, he gave me this dire warning.'

'What dire warning?'

'Well, he sucked the air through his two front teeth and he wrinkled up his nose and he scratched at his crutch and he said, if I stayed here, I'd turn into a shrivelled little dried-out runt of an old man and I'd button up my cardigan in the wrong holes. I'd be forever wearing my socks inside out. I'd have a permanent dewdrop on the end of my nose. I'd end up fearfully benign, fearfully batty.

'And I thought about it, Rosie.

'I thought about it hour after hour as I sat in the lavatory staring at my thumbnails. And then it came to me in a flash. How wonderful. How marvellous. That is exactly what I want to be when I grow up – I want to be like Father.'

'Yes,' said Rosie softly.

'I want to be like Father now.'

'Yes.'

'Just look at him, rambling away to himself, covering himself with sparks and blinking like a self-satisfied toad. Fearfully benign, Rosie. Fearfully batty.'

Father flicked at another wasp and chuckled to himself.

'In India, when you die they bung you on top of this whacking great pyre,' he said. 'And then they burn you and . . .'

He chuckled again and prodded at a burning ember of tobacco on the front of his navy-blue-and-white houndstooth trousers.

'Pyre,' he said. 'What a lovely word. Pyre. Higher and higher went the pyre. And they set the pyre on fire. Pyre. Fearfully pleasant word.'

He dozed off again.

A jackdaw strutted sideways along the roof ridge of the old stables. In its beak it held a fragment of silver paper. Its eyes glinted.

'I don't want to travel the world, Rosie,' said William. 'I don't want to have adventures.'

'I know, William, I know. You're quite content writing your books about railways, aren't you?'

'Yes.'

'Just think of all the pleasure you bring to people writing about marshalling yards and signal gantries and points and junctions and . . .'

'There's no need to be sarky.'

'I'm not being sarky.'

'You are.'

'I'm not.'

William clenched his fists and stamped his feet. Rosie's face turned scarlet and her nostrils flared.

The helicopter returned, clattering low over the rooftops of the village. The jackdaw dropped its fragment of silver paper and with a *zack zacker zack* of alarm flew away into the shrubbery.

Father opened one eye and said:

'There goes another. The tenth today. Whacko. Jolly Dee.'

32

At long last we were alone together, Winston and I.

The water gushed and rilled through the runnels of the old stone trout hatchery. The shire horse cropped the grass peacefully in Cuckoo Tree Meadow. The barn owl hunted the first flickers of dusk.

We were sitting side by side on an old log blown down by long-distant winter gales.

The distant gales of my childhood.

Rosie screaming in her cot. Ailsa Craig beating back the gulls in a force ten storm. Mother and Father at it hammer and tongs in the front parlour of that narrow, haughty house in Hunstanton and William huddled deep into my chest and sobbing. Storms and tempests and always the warm flickering candle of my heart.

I turned to Winston and said:

'I'd got such wonderful plans for us, Winston.'

'That you had, Nancy,' he said warmly. 'That you had without a shadow of a doubt, my old wingsy bash.'

'We were going to set up home together, you and I, Winston. We were going to live somewhere nice.'

'But it's nice here, Nancy. I was born in this village look. I knows every nook and cranny of the neighbourhood round here for miles and miles sort of thing. There's not a pub in the district what ain't seen old Winston having a sesh and a good old neck and a grope with one of his bits of fluff.'

'Winston!'

'Sorry, Nancy, sorry.'

He took out his old battered tin box and rolled himself a cigarette. He licked the end with the tip of his juicy pink tongue. The match spurted and flared. He inhaled deeply. He sighed with contentment.

The contentment of my distant childhood.

Weekends with Grandpapa in the old schoolhouse in Devon. Hiding in the bracken to watch the wild ponies suckling their foals. Ravens wheeling high above the tors. Grandmama and her bosom. Just me. Just Nancy and her grandpapa and his starched wing collar and her grandmama and her hairy nose.

Winston sighed deeply again and said:

'See that old trout hatchery yonder, Nancy?'

'Yes.'

'Well, that's where I learned all the arts and the skills and the wiles of poaching.'

'Is it, Winston?'

'Oh yes, missus. Without a doubt.'

His eyes misted over and the faint evening breeze snatched gingerly at the locks of hair coiling over the collar of his open-necked shirt.

He was like a great smouldering bonfire lighting up the dark, lonely shadows of my childhood.

He chuckled to himself and said:

'When I was a little lad before I got all hirsute and rampant sort of thing, I used to lie in the bushes here all quiet and silent, looking out on Mother Nature doing her business all undisturbed and innocent.

'Cor blimey Charlie, I seen sights, Nancy.

'Kingfishers diving for minnows with scarcely a plop or a ripple. Herons, stilty-legged and hungry eyes and stabbing beaks. Mink skulking through the reeds snapping the heads off moorhen chicks. Betty Hayballs swimming in the salmon pool with nothing on but her black daps when she thought no one was looking. By the cringe, even at that age she'd got a rare old king-sized pair on her.'

'Thank you very much, Winston,' I said sharply. 'That's quite enough of that, thank you.'

But I couldn't help smiling, and my heart leapt like a salmon and I longed to nip his neck like a mink skulking in the reeds.

'Sorry, Nancy, sorry,' he said.

The barn owl set out his white flag in the lengthening dusk. But the sun still shone low over the sweep of the distant Downs and its rays soothed away the thinness of my misery.

'I used to come courting my missus down here look,' said Winston. 'We'd lie down side by side hidden by that clump of old teasels yonder, and we'd share a Players Weight and then I'd roll down her wellies and take out her teeth sort of thing and we'd . . .'

'Where did you first meet your wife, Winston?' I said hastily.

'At the village fete, Nancy. She'd come to stay with her uncle, the retired arsonist. Well, she was the star attraction, wasn't she?'

'What of?'

'Well, you knows that stall where you throws a ball and, if you hits the target, it propels an ugly woman out of bed and shoots her into a bath of cold water?'

'Yes.'

'Well, my missus was the ugly woman, Nancy. She was the ugliest woman they'd ever had in the whole history of the fete look. They was queuing up in droves to hurl balls at her. So was I. You couldn't keep me away. And I hit the target every time. And out she shot from that old bed with a shriek and a scream and in she fell into the bath like a bloody great blubbery walrus. It was love at first sight.'

'But why?'

'I've always wanted to marry an ugly woman, Nancy. You marry an ugly woman, and you've got every excuse for having your bits of fluff on the side. Stands to reason, don't it? You get everybody's sympathy look. They encourages you. The bits of fluff are hammering at your door to . . .'

He stopped, took hold of my hand and said urgently:

'Nancy.'

'Yes, Winston?'

'I don't think you're an ugly woman, Nancy.'

'No?'

'No. I thinks you're a very beautiful woman, Nancy. Handsome. Tasty. Desirable. Great pair of berdongers.'

'Oh, Winston,' I said, squeezing his hand and feeling my berdongers, my breasts, swell with pride and love.

'If anyone ever suggests you should lie in bed and have balls thrown at you at the village fete, I'll punch his bloody head in. That I will without a doubt.'

How lovely to be fought over, I thought.

How delicious to have two grown men fighting for your honour. Rosemary Wilkinson from the tennis club in Wilmslow once had three chaps from the Colts cricket team rolling round in the car park fighting for her . . .

Bugger Rosemary Wilkinson.

I laughed and clasped hold of Winston's hands and placed them to my chin. 'Oh, Winston,' I said. 'We could have had such a lovely lovely time together.'

'I knows, Nancy.'

'We could have lived in Lyme Regis. Near the sea. Near the shops. I'm not known in Lyme Regis, you see and . . .

'Nancy.'

'Yes, Winston?'

'Why couldn't we set up home in your place here in Winterleaf Gunner?'

'Because I have a certain status here, Winston,' I said. 'I've got a position. I've got appearances to keep up and . . .'

Oh, Nancy, Nancy, the cock crowed thrice.

I felt so ashamed.

I stroked the back of his gnarled old scarred brown hands and I said:

'What's the point of talking about it, Winston? It's all over now. Father's not going to die. Rosie's staying. William's staying. And, therefore, Nancy's staying. Of course. Naturally. What would they do without Nancy? How could they possibly survive without Nancy?'

Winston sucked in deeply through the blue-chipped gap in his two front teeth. Then he guffawed and he said:

'Tell you what we'll do, Nancy.'

'What?'

'We'll be all romantic. We'll get into my motor, my car, and we'll elope.'

'What?'

'We'll piss off to . . .'

'Winston! Will you please stop using that dreadful language?'

He hung his head.

'Sorry, Nancy,' he said balefully. 'I got carried away. Forget what I just said. Stupid – that's what it was. Stupid without a doubt sort of thing.'

'No, Winston. No. I think it's a marvellous idea.'

'You does?'

'Of course I do.'

Instantly the skies cleared. The storm clouds scudded away over the sun-brimmed horizon. The tempest abated and the still waters sparkled and kingfishers plunged with scarcely a plop, scarcely a ripple.

I clapped my hands together and I cried out:

'We'll elope tonight. I'll go to the dry cleaners straightaway and collect my tweed suit. Then I'll buy a couple of new toothbrushes from the chemist's and some powder for your feet. Then I'll . . .'

'Wait a minute, Nancy,' said Winston. 'Hold your horses. Not so fast. We got to take our time.'

'Take our time? Why?'

'We wants to get our revenge on them, Nancy.'

'Revenge? What on earth are you talking about, Winston?'

'We wants to punish them for all the terrible things what they've done to you over the years. We wants to make them see themselves as they really are. So we lulls them, Nancy.'

'We lulls them, Winston?'

'Yes, we lulls them so they don't suspect a thing. They thinks everything's back to normal look. All hunky dory. All safe, sound and secure. And then at that moment, Nancy, we pounces.'

'We pounces, Winston? But how?'

'Oh, you leave that to old Winston, Nancy. I ain't the village poacher and part-time philosopher for nothing, you know. That I ain't without a doubt. I knows what to do, Nancy. You just sit tight and leave everything to old Winston.'

And he winked.

And he laughed.

And he sucked in deeply through the gap in his teeth.

And then quite without warning he kissed me full on the lips.

And he touched me.

He ran his hands all over my body and he said:

'Cor, Nancy, cor. I knows I was talking all enthusiastic sort of thing about Betty Hayballs and the size of her berdongers but . . .'

'That's quite enough of that, thank you, Winston,' I said.

And then I kissed him back full on the lips and said:

'That's quite enough – until the next time.'

33

I walked home alone from the trout hatchery.

I was plump with happiness.

Revenge? What did he mean by that?

Who cared?

I was happy, I was content.

I had a man. My man. And he wasn't a shaveling from the tennis club hops. He wasn't a stiff, fumbling innocent like my poor dead Geoffrey of long, long ago.

He could hold the whole of summer in the palms of his hands. He could suck in the icy blast of winter through the blue-chipped gap in his two front teeth and keep me free of the frosts and crackling ice of my misery.

When he touched me on the river bank and the barn owl ghosted the reeds, he held the whole of my summer in his gentle, loving hands.

That evening we settled ourselves round the dinner table. Rosie was wearing her purple mohair jumper with the floppy collar and jeans. I wanted to say something about wearing trousers at dinner, but I held my peace.

William was wearing his oatmeal cardigan. I wanted to say something about ripping it from his back and stuffing it inch by inch up his nostrils, but I held my peace.

Father reamed his pipe contentedly with the Georgian silver pickle fork Mother had won at bowls in Eastbourne all those years ago.

Rosie sniffed her disapproval.

And William tapped impatiently on the table with his soup spoon.

'Come on, Winston,' he said. 'Come on, old chap. I wonder what he's serving up tonight?'

'Well, if it's anything as good as last night's effort, it'll be absolutely delicious,' I said.

'I know, I know,' said William. 'Eggs mimosa. Loin of lamb with plum compote. That plum compote! I had at least six helpings.'

'How disgusting,' snarled Rosie. 'How revoltingly gluttonous.'

'It is not gluttonous.'

'It is.'

'It isn't.'

'It is is is is is.'

Father sucked the end of the pickle fork, wiped it on a corner of the tablecloth and said:

'I once knew a chap who died of gluttony. He was an aviator in the Sind. He died of a surfeit of Basmati rice and Tizer. He used to fly exceedingly low and loop the loop. Strange fellow. He came from Forfar. Or was it Edgbaston?'

I was longing for Winston to arrive with dinner.

But I was nervous, too.

Revenge?

What did he mean by revenge?

When we were at the trout hatchery that evening there had been a fervour in his voice. There'd been spikes of cruelty, too, which I'd never detected in him before.

Oh yes, he was rough and ready. He was coarse and vulgar. His ablutions habits were quite ghastly and goodness knows what the ladies from flower arranging at Lyme Regis would have made of him.

But cruelty? No. I'd never looked upon Winston as a cruel man.

My heart fluttered as I waited for him.

He always looked so handsome when he served us dinner.

He'd have slicked back his hair. He'd be wearing an alpaca jacket and pinstriped trousers and black patent leather dancing pumps. And his shirt would be crispy white and . . .

Suddenly the door burst open and Winston kicked in the trolley.

It crashed and it clattered.

And then he stepped inside.

173

'Winston!' cried Rosie.

'Good God, man, what are you wearing?' cried William.

It was not a pleasant sight.

Winston was wearing a damp brown balaclava encrusted with pigeon droppings.

His coarse khaki shirt was streaked with oil and mouldering patches of offal and it was open to his hairy navel.

His corduroy trousers were tied below the knee with sisal and his wellington boots were flapping at his ankles and shining with dung.

'Winston, what on earth do you think you're playing at?' said Rosie and her jaw jutted and her eyes blazed.

Winston disregarded her gaze and said offhandedly:

'Serving your dinner, ain't I?'

'Whacko, old boy. Jolly Dee,' said Father. 'What is it tonight? Something fearfully scrumptious, eh?'

'Oh yes. Without a doubt,' said Winston. 'Egg and chips and stewed fig pudding with lumpy custard. And you'll have to do the washing-up yourselves on account of the simple fact that I'm off to the pub for a sesh, and if you manages to eat all your fig pudding I'd make sure you got a good supply of bog roll in for the night to come.

'Right then, I'll bid you goodnight. And I'd eat your nosh quick before it gets any more colder than what it is already. I learned that from books, see.'

And with that he left us, slamming the door violently behind him so that the old carriage clock juddered on the mantelpiece and made tiny, wheezing, complaining noises deep in its innards.

We stared at each other speechless.

The chips withered before our eyes. The eggs congealed. The thick leathery skin on the surface of the custard puckered and festered.

Father tapped out his pipe into the fig pudding. Then he looked up and smiled.

'We could always have sardines on toast,' he said. 'Fearfully pleasant, sardines – provided you can manage to open the tin.'

I went into the kitchen and made us corned beef sandwiches in stale bread. William and Rosie quarrelled violently over the selection of programmes on the television, and Rosie left the room in a raging temper and William sat on the piano stool and sulked and rattled his ball bearings.

Father continued his story about the aviator from the Sind only it was Kashmir and he came from Lanarkshire and died in a bus accident in Dartford or was it Monmouth?

I sat silent with my knitting, brooding.

What on earth was Winston up to? What plans was he hatching? What spells and magic was he going to weave round us? What turmoil and tribulation was he going to bring to our lives?

That night I heard him return from the pub in his motor, his car.

He drove into the dustbins, and they clanked and crumpled. He reversed into the laurel and its branches rasped and clawed angrily at the roof of his car.

The door slammed. Winston stumbled out and fell on his knees in the gravel. He heaved himself upright, and then he began to sing at the top of his voice.

I stood by the window, pressed close to the cold, comfortless wall, peering out through a gap in the curtains.

Winston was standing there, shirt wrapped round his waist, his belly dripping with waddies of stale beer, his flies undone, the laces flapping from his boots, and he was swatting at the moths with his damp brown balaclava.

And then he stopped.

And he shouted at the top of his voice at the moon:

'Just like a walrus.

'Just like a bloody great fat walrus.'

Next morning I caught him scurrying along the corridor towards William's study.

'Winston, what on earth is going on?' I said.

'Ah, don't you worry your arse about it, Nancy,' he said.

'Keep calm, my old wingsy bash. Keep cool. Just you leave it all to old Winston.'

And with that he winked, tapped the side of his nose, kissed me full on the lips and whispered:

'You and me together, eh, Nancy? You and me alone in a great heaving roaring bucking bed.'

Winston left Nancy Empson open-mouthed and speechless and entered William's study without knocking on the door.

'Hullo, William,' he said. 'Not disturbing you, am I?'

William spun round from his typewriter with a start and said: 'What?'

'I said, William – not disturbing you, am I?'

'Well, it is rather inconvenient really, Winston. I'm just getting to the crux of my book, the nub and I'm – I say, do you mind not playing with my stapling machine.'

Winston tossed the stapling machine on to the desk and said:

'Mucky book, is it, William?'

'What?'

'The book you're writing. Is he mucky?'

'No, it is not. How dare you?' said William, flushing angrily. 'This is a monograph on the Manchester, South Junction and Altrincham Railway and . . .'

Before he could finish his sentence, Winston had ripped the sheet of paper from the typewriter and was studying it quizzically, sucking in through the gap in his two front teeth.

'What the devil do you think you're doing,' William said.

Winston smiled broadly and said:

'Having a look at what you been writing, William.'

'Give it here.'

Winston held the sheet of paper above his head out of reach of William's frantically, feebly, scrabbling hands.

'Now, now, William,' he said. 'Don't snatch. You'll tear him, won't you?'

William sank back into his chair and said weakly:

'What are you doing, Winston?'

'Now there's no need to get alarmed, William. I ain't a savage, you know. I likes books. I've read them all in my time look. Virginia Woolf. Thomas Love Peacock. Honoré de Balzac. *The Playfair Football Annual*.

'Oh yes, William, old Winston knows a good book when he sees one. And that is without a shadow of a doubt.'

He straightened out the sheet of paper with a flick of his wrists, screwed up his eyes and said:

'Now then, let's see what you've wrote here, shall we?'

He peered intently at the paper, sucking in his breath and nodding slowly to himself.

Then he began to read out loud:

' "The opening of Knott Mill Station proved to be a watershed in the fortunes of the Manchester, South Junction and Altrincham Railway." '

He looked up and smiled.

'Beautiful, William,' he said. 'A fine stylistic touch, if I might say so. Let's read on, eh?'

He held out the paper at arm's length with a flourish and a jaunty tilt to his head, and he read on:

' "Troubles with rolling stock, particularly the twenty-five elderly six-wheelers of LNWR design built at Wolverton, had caused severe curtailment of services on ..." '

He looked up and sighed deeply.

'Curtailment, eh?' he said. 'Very nice, William. You got a real way with words, ain't you? They just flows and lilts over the paper, don't they?'

'Give it me back, Winston,' said William plaintively. 'Please, please.'

'Certainly, William, certainly,' said Winston and he handed over the paper with a deep bow.

Then he smiled and said:

'And I'll tell you something else what might interest you.'

'What's that?'

'You've spelled Wolverton wrong look. Yes, William, my old wingsy bash, you've spelled him wrong.'

He picked up the stapling machine, put it to his ear, shook it and said:

'And you ain't got no staples in this machine neither – pathetic little twat.'

William was almost crying when he told me what had happened.

I was appalled. I was outraged.

Oh, I knew he was a pathetic little twat. I'd been telling him that all his life. Not in so many words. I'd always tried to be kind and sympathetic and considerate.

'You're a hopeless, helpless, congenital, incurable drip, William,' I used to say.

But that was me talking, his sister. I most certainly was not going to let outsiders get in on the act.

I resolved to have it out with Winston there and then.

But he was nowhere to be found.

I looked into the utility room. I looked into the kitchen. I looked into the old stables where Winston had set up his workshop.

But there was no sign of him.

Where was he skulking? Where was he hiding? What was he hatching up for us?

That afternoon I took my sewing into the garden and sat with Father who was stretched out in the hammock Winston had made for him in the spring from an army parachute which he told us was 'surplus to requirements sort of thing'.

Father puffed at his pipe.

His panama hat was pulled down over his eyes.

He was awash with contentment.

'I remember once visiting Jewtown in Cochin.'

'Do you, Father?' I said, and instinctively I braced myself for another one of his interminable stories.

Those stories! When had they started? Had they always been with us like an old dog that bumps into the furniture and stares at you silently with dull rheumy eyes and refuses to budge when you try to pass him on the stairs?

Did he tell those stories when Mother was still with us? Did they start after she'd gone? I didn't remember. For years and years they'd entwined themselves like devil's garter in the rhythms of my life, strangling and suffocating.

Those stories! How on earth could we survive without them?

'Curious, isn't it? Jews in India,' said Father. 'You don't expect to find Jews in the subcontinent. Cricketers – yes. Bank managers. Dog trainers. Typewriter engineers. Egg packers. But it comes as quite a shock to find Jews.

'Anyway, I went to Jewtown in Cochin with Mr Bannerjee from the wine merchant's and we took a taxi from the station, sharing, of course, and we wended our way through the narrow, chattering streets and presently we found ourselves in this shaded square with very old women sitting on crumbling dry stone walls chewing leaves, and the skinny native dogs snuffled in the refuse.'

On and on he went.

I dozed over my sewing.

Wasps droned. Doves cooed and gurgled into their chests. The sun snoozed behind the haze.

And then Winston appeared.

He was wearing his alpaca jacket and his pin-striped trousers. His hair was slicked back and he was bearing a silver tray on which were dishes of black olives and pickled gherkins and two slender glasses filled to the brim with Madeira.

'Hullo, Nancy,' he said. 'What do you reckon? Not a lot. Oh my God – there goes your old dad. Telling another of them bollock-rotting stories of his, is he?'

'Winston!' I gasped.

'Boring old fart. He wants to . . .'

'Winston!' I shouted. 'How dare you talk to my father like that?'

He cackled. It was a most unsavoury cackle, too.

'You wants to throw a bucket of water over him, missus,' he said. 'I'd throw a bucket of water over him and then I'd put him out of his misery like what you does with an old carthorse what stands in the stables all day trumping incessant and eating up all your nosh.'

And with that he drank the two glasses of Madeira in a single gulp, winked at me, turned on his heel and trotted back to the house singing to himself.

I was speechless.

My whole body quivered with rage. Every nerve end jangled. And Father smiled and nodded and said:

'Fearfully pleasant cove, Winston. Reminds me of a native coastguard I once knew in Calicut. Or was it . . . No, it was definitely Calicut. I say, Nancy, old boy, I've got it right.'

What was his game?

What on earth was Winston up to?

I locked myself in my sewing room. I paced up and down. I forgot all about my appointment at the hairdresser. I forgot to take my mid-afternoon vitamin C pill. I forgot . . .

Then suddenly it hit me.

Of course. Of course.

It was I who was Winston's victim.

It was me he was lulling.

It was me he was going to take his revenge on.

Of course. Of course.

It was the perfect way to rid himself of me and my attentions. Pretend he was going to elope with me. Pretend he was playing this devious, subtle game to turn the family against him.

And all the time he was turning me against him, so I'd throw him out of the house, dismiss him out of my life, and he could slink away scot-free without a second of guilt and with all the world on his side.

The wronged, innocent village poacher led astray by a foolish, love-sick spinster lady of mature years.

Of course. Of course.

And then I looked out of the window and saw Winston leading Rosie by the hand to his motor, his car.

He was dressed in his navy-blue corduroy suit and his yellow cravat with the red fox heads.

And Rosie had her blonde hair swept back and held in place with a pink velvet ribbon.

They drove off.

But of course. Of course.

Whilst Nancy Empson was fretting in her sewing room Winston was settling Rosie in the pub with the ornamental herons and the tropical birds.

'You likes it here, don't you, Rosie?'

'Yes, Winston, I do. It's lovely.'

Winston settled himself on a wooden bench next to her and said:

'You're the only one of my bits of fluff what I ever brought here, Rosie,' he said.

'I know,' said Rosie. 'You told me when you first brought me here. And I was very flattered.'

'Good,' said Winston stroking his chin thoughtfully. 'Do you remember what happened that day, Rosie?'

'Yes,' said Rosie and she smiled radiantly. 'You told me that you loved me. And I was very touched, very moved.'

'Good,' said Winston. 'Good.'

He sipped slowly at his pint of scrumpy. He rolled himself a cigarette and then he said:

'Rosie, I got something else to tell you on the same subject sort of thing.'

'Well, tell me, Winston. Don't be shy. Tell me.'

'Right,' said Winston. 'I don't love you. I never have loved you. I thinks you're a self-centred, vain, foul-tempered, spoilt little cow bag.'

'What?'

'And as for that Nancy. Well, as for that Nancy . . .'

Later that evening Rosie came storming into my bedroom.

Her eyes were flashing. Her lips were quivering, her face was flushed and her hair was awry.

In a gabble and a torrent she told me what Winston had said to her in the pub.

The things he had said about her!

The things he had said about me!

She sobbed in my arms. Her whole body shook and pumped.

I stroked her hair.

I kissed her cheeks.

I fondled her and I comforted her.

'Rosie, Rosie,' I whispered. 'Don't cry, my darling. Don't upset yourself.'

'The things he said, Nancy,' sobbed Rosie. 'The awful, terrible things he said.'

'There, there, Rosie,' I said. 'It's all over now. No more, my darling. No more.'

And I meant it.

Oh, brother, did I mean it.

34

Next morning I called an emergency family conference.

We gathered in the drawing room.

The plump sun leaned its back smugly against the doors of the french windows.

A magpie cackled. The green woodpecker yaffled.

'Right then,' I said. 'You all know why we're gathered here, I presume.'

'Haven't a clue, old boy,' said Father. 'It's not another of those fearful family conflabs, is it?'

'Yes, it is, Father,' said Rosie.

'Oh lor,' said Father. 'Well, don't bother to wake me up, when I fall asleep. Take my vote as read, will you?'

The conference did not take long. We each had our say.

'I think Winston should go immediately,' said William. 'Why he was ever allowed to stay in the first place I shall never know. I blame you, Rosie.'

'Me? What's it got to do with me? It was you who . . .'

'Rosie, William,' I screamed. 'Shut up. Shut up.'

'Sorry, Nancy,' said Rosie softly.

She hesitated for a moment, and then she said firmly.

'I think he should go.'

'And so do I,' I said. 'Right. That's it. I shall go and tell him at once. He'll be out of this house before noon.'

I wasn't frightened.

Not in the least bit.

I felt excited.

Thank God, I had found out before he made a complete and utter fool of me.

How could I have been so stupid? How could I have demeaned myself so? How could I have been so gullible, so innocent?

I found Winston in the utility room.

He was lying asleep in the humpbacked armchair Mother had bought in Bridlington or was it Barnstaple? On the table beside him was a half empty bottle of whisky. I kicked him hard on the shins and shouted:

'Right, you. On your feet.'

He gasped and spluttered, but when he saw me, his eyes lit up and he said:

'Oh, Nancy. What do you reckon then?'

'Not a lot, Winston,' I said. 'Nothing at all in fact. Right then, on your hind legs. And out! This instant. Sling your hook. Get out of this house at once.'

'You what, Nancy?'

'How dare you behave in this way. You disgusting, sickening, filthy, arrogant, beer-swilling, scrumpy-sodden, belly-flopping bastard.

'So I'm mutton dressed as lamb, am I? I'm a frustrated old spinster. I'm a love-lorn, repressed old snob just out for a bit of rough on the sly. I'm a . . . I'm a . . .'

He began to laugh.

He threw back his head and roared and bellowed and rocked with laughter.

I couldn't stop myself.

I launched myself at him.

I kicked him. I thrashed at him with my fists. I bit him. I scratched him.

And he went on laughing.

He laughed and he laughed and he laughed.

And almost casually he took hold of my arms and pinned them behind my back.

And he kissed me. He kissed me full on the lips. He fondled me. And I did not fight back. I just crumpled up into his chest. And I whispered:

'Oh, Winston, Winston, Winston.'

Winston kissed my neck. He kissed my breasts. He buried his face into my hair.

And then he said:

'You see, Nancy. I told you to trust old Winston. It's all worked out look.'

'How?'

'My plans have succeeded. First the family against me. Then you turns against me. You gets your dander up with me, you turfs me out of the house, and they doesn't suspect a thing.'

'What?'

'They doesn't suspect a thing, Nancy, my old wingsy bash. They hasn't a single, solitary notion about what you and I feels for each other.'

'No?'

'Course they don't, Nancy. So it's all set up now. You and me.'

He pressed me closer to him and I ran my fingers through his long greasy coils of hair and purred my lips over the curve and droop of his Zapata moustache.

'I loves you, Nancy. I desires you. I wants you. I needs you.'

'And I you, Winston,' I said.

Suddenly he bellowed with laughter again.

'Right then, we're all ready to go, missus. The day of the autumn fete – that's when we'll elope. They'll all be there. So you get yourself ready and all dicky-dolled up, and old Winston'll come to collect you in his motor, his car look, and off we'll go, you and me together, Nancy, for a new life of fancy free and rampant lovey dovey. I loves you, Nancy. I loves you.'

And this time I believed him.

I really believed him.

35

The day of the autumn fete dawned bright and clear.

Rosie, William and Father went off to work on the stalls.

Well, it was hardly work as far as Father was concerned. He was going to the pub to supervise supplies of gin for Mrs Fokins on the hoopla stall.

I excused myself for a moment. I said that as Winston had been thrown out, I had to do all the housework and some urgent washing and ironing.

They did not suspect a thing as they trooped happily out of the house.

I paused at the front door, watching them scrunch away over the gravel.

I could hear the band playing in the distance.

My happy family! Would I miss them? Would I miss Rosie and her long, glowing blonde hair and the sweetness of her smile when she was happy and the way she licked the end of her nose with her tongue when she was concentrating? Would I miss William in his oatmeal cardigan and his Cheshire Lines Railway bow tie and his simple joys and his simple pleasures and the soft pout of his lips when he kissed me goodnight? Would I miss Father and his MCC spats and his bottle-green plus fours and the merry twinkle in his eye and the sadness of his stories and the warmth in his voice when he called me 'old boy'?

Would I hell as like.

Would I buggery.

Quickly I packed my belongings.

Not everything.

I packed my tweed suit and the summer dresses I'd bought from that ghastly lady with the buck teeth and the hooked nose at the Oxfam shop last winter.

I packed the picture of Mother at Balmoral and the book of Rudyard Kipling stories Father had given me for my ninth birthday all those years ago when we lived in Herne Bay.

I packed the . . .

And then there was a knock on the door.

I dashed downstairs.

I opened the door.

And there was Winston.

And I knew what he was going to say.

'Sorry, Nancy. It's all off.'

'I see.'

'I can't go with you Nancy.'

'I see.'

'Sit down, Nancy. Sit on the step next to me and let me tell you all quiet and calm sort of thing.'

His voice was calm.

I was calm, too.

Me? Nancy? Calm?

Dear God.

I sat down on the step beside him. I stared straight ahead. The laurel looked at me haughtily, disdainfully, mockingly.

Winston coughed and his voice was still calm when he said:

'I went to the fete just for a last look round. I saw your old dad knocking back gin at the back of the hoopla stall. I saw William on the home-produce stall signing his railway books. I saw Rosie on the bring-and-buy stall arguing with Nansen Ticehurst.

'And then I saw my wife, my missus.

'She was lying on this bed look. And underneath her was this whacking great bath full of cold water. So I thinks to myself – why not? Just one last throw for old time's sake. And I placed the ball in my hand. I took careful aim, Nancy. I hurled it with all my might. And it landed spot on target, and out she fell into the bath with a bloody great splash and everyone cheered and everyone hollered and I thought ... I thought ...

'I thought my heart's turning over.

'It's turning over just like the first time I ever set eyes on her.

'And I knew I could never leave her, Nancy.

'I knew it was always ordained that I should live with an ugly woman.

'Not with you, Nancy. You're a beautiful woman. You're a tasty woman, handsome and I desires you and I wants you and I loves you.'

I didn't say a thing.

My whole mind was empty. My body was empty. I had no past, no present, no future.

I allowed Winston to take me by the hand and lead me in to his motor, in to his car.

He drove me to the wood at the back of his house.

He took me to the beech tree where we had first made love on the day of the village fete in last year's long and drowsy summer.

We lay down side by side.

He kissed me. He fondled me.

'I loves you, Nancy,' he said. 'I really loves you. And this is the best way I knows of showing it.'

'Winston, Winston,' I sighed.

'It's going to be good, Nancy. Just the same as it was before. You with your family. Me with my ugly wife. And you and me together under a great beech tree, kissing and cuddling and sharing the joys of our bodies. This is the best way, Nancy. This is the best way of all. I loves you, Nancy. I really loves you.'

And I believed him.

I believed him totally and overwhelmingly.

He wrapped himself around me.

I felt his presence.

All of it, firm and strong and just for me.

And I groaned.

I cried out.

I arched my back and I cried out long and loud.

After a while an army helicopter roared low overhead.

I did not attempt to cover myself.

I just looked up and said:

'I say, Winston, a helicopter. Whacko. Jolly Dee.'
Oh yes.
Oh yes, we are what is called a happy family.
Without a shadow of a doubt sort of thing.